Guano

A NOVEL

LOUIS CARMAIN

TRANSLATED BY RHONDA MULLINS

COACH HOUSE BOOKS, TORONTO

First English edition. Originally published in French in 2013 as *Guano* by Les Éditions de l'Hexagone.

 Canada Council **Conseil des Arts**
for the Arts **du Canada**    ONTARIO ARTS COUNCIL
CONSEIL DES ARTS DE L'ONTARIO
an Ontario government agency
un organisme du gouvernement de l'Ontario   **Canadä**

We acknowledge the financial support of the Government of Canada through the National Translation Program for Book Publishing, an initiative of the *Roadmap for Canada's Official Languages 2013–2018: Education, Immigration, Communities*, for our translation activities. Published with the generous assistance of the Canada Council for the Arts and the Ontario Arts Council. Coach House Books also acknowledges the support of the Government of Canada through the Canada Book Fund.

LIBRARY AND ARCHIVES CANADA CATALOGUING IN PUBLICATION

Carmain, Louis, 1983-
[Guano. English]
        Guano / Louis Carmain ; Rhonda Mullins, translator.

Translation of: Guano.
Issued in print and electronic formats.
ISBN 978-1-55245-315-5 (paperback)

        I. Mullins, Rhonda, 1966-, translator II. Title. III. Title: Guano. English.

PS8605.A7558G8213 2015   C843'.6   C2015-905044-8

Guano is available as an ebook: ISBN 978 1 77056 424 4

Because after all, if literature is not a collection of
femmes fatales and creatures on the road to ruin,
it's not worth reading.

— Julien Gracq

Pinzón

1862–1863

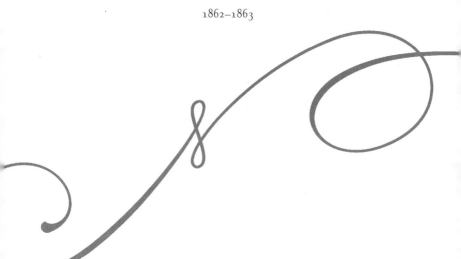

1

This is a story of love and war. Since both diversions often spring from the most trivial of things – borders strained, smiles exchanged – and, to everyone's astonishment, turn into much more – death, tears, other surprises – there was nothing particularly remarkable at the beginning.

A city in the background, a port in foreground – such is Cadix. In six years' time, a revolution will become part of the landscape, but for the time being, there are just a few preparations and their fallout. Two Spanish navy ships, seagulls circling the masts, twice as many men as seagulls. Twice as many, and half of them are bare chested and carrying barrels, cannonballs, butterfly nets and grapeshot, jumbled together with a pile of lenses, magnifying glasses and a *Systema Naturae*. They are indiscriminately loading nails and insect pins with undoubtedly interchangeable uses. Nearby, scientists beg the handlers to make the necessary distinctions (a setting block is not a gangplank) and perhaps even to discern (nor is a microscope a telescope), to be gentler as they hold the fates of a botanist indisposed by the August heat and a herbarium in their hands.

All the same, some must assume their rank: the admiral, the captains, a minister of Her Majesty. Indeed, they are wearing frogged uniforms with épaulettes so broad they tempt the pigeons, the men all cinched and strapped in, making either chests or paunches more prominent, depending on the regimen. They are sweating more than the seamen.

Bare chest to the wind, navel free.

Gentlemen, we can dream.

The minister mops his brow with a navy blue handkerchief. What a sun, Admiral, the very idea of the sun. Would you agree that the moon is preferable, the mere memory of the sun? Its melancholy, its gentleness, its craters offering proof that it wears no makeup. The admiral has thick eyebrows that jut out like awnings, protecting his eyes from the drips. Do you wax them?

We'll come back to that. It was a bit of a non sequitur.

The lieutenants, a thankless rank, offer a bit of help hauling cargo, assuming their station for a moment, the deck, then the dock, then the deck. Finally they break rank completely, roll up their sleeves and leave their cocked hats on the edge of the jetties. Let's pick up the pace.

The doñas and their ladies-in-waiting eye the torsos and uniforms. The barrels, not so much. A parasol hides their eyes, a hand hides their mouth. It's hard to hear what they are whispering: an aesthetic appraisal, a verdict of ugliness, don't go, sweet Roberto. The rising sun stretches the indistinct shadows of these dissimilar women as far as the docks, equality being found in the shadowy shapes and the longing, and extends the shadows' black peaks – to which the rigging adds a lacy touch – as far as the water. The sailors step on the shadows as they work, provoking a frisson in their owners ... a transposition, a secret desire. They excuse themselves, needlessly, afraid that the ladies' only memory of them will be an indiscretion. After all, who knows when they will see these familiar silhouettes again? So many *au revoirs* become *adieus*.

And suddenly Spain is too beautiful to leave. That's the way it is with adventure: when it becomes real, when the time comes to take to the seas, suddenly we are better suited to our slippers.

❧

It was Isabelle II who had dreamed up this particular adventure, albeit steered a little in the direction by her government. She has been on the throne for nineteen years and feels entitled to her whims.

She is very much of her time: pale skin, black hair, more than pleasingly plump. Her exile in Paris lies six years ahead of her, when her chin will grow fourfold.

At the time our story begins, people are still merely grumbling in the corridors about the virtues of her reign. She is growing fatter at the expense of Spain, whose weight on the world stage is dwindling. She has a penchant for intrigue and French cuisine. She has too many small dogs. And yet, under her reign, Spain is once again the fourth greatest naval power, and military spending is more than respectable.

Isabelle is doing everything possible – in other words, she is doing something at least. But it all lacks fanfare and sizzle. People are searching for prestige lost and not finding it. Castilian dignitaries demand a red carpet wherever they go; it's not too much to ask. Instead, in the courts of Europe, they are received as a courtesy between a businessman's grievances and a Turkish emissary's ultimatums. Questionable wines follow half-hearted bows, accompanied by a glaring lack of nubile heiresses. And then there are the newspapers in London, Rome and Moscow, where Spain is relegated to mere snippets – even in the Madrid papers.

So Isabelle, suddenly thirsty for knowledge, had the idea of mounting a scientific expedition. Destination: the waters of South America, a continent that has been all the rage since Darwin. People now know it as a destination where rare birds chirp, the latest fish swim, ten-thousand-year-old lizards do, well, not much of anything. And, while we're there, we can collect some of the money that the newly independent colonies – not to name names – owe the crown. While we're at it, we can discreetly throw our weight behind the legal and financial demands of Spanish citizens still living there. It is a question of honour. But, above all, it is a question of science, lest we forget, of two-headed tortoises, five-legged salamanders, chaffinches with teeth, and if a geologist were to find some leftover gold lying about, so much the better.

$\mathcal{A}$

The admiral with the awnings is Luís Hernandez Pinzón. He commands the fleet with no great distinction. He is a direct descendant of the brothers Pinzón, who accompanied Christopher Columbus on that other voyage (a lineage that makes him uncertain of the value of his admiralty), and his bloodline will show those people overseas that Spain is not messing about. It will show them that the expedition will revolutionize the world of science as surely as that other one revolutionized the world, full stop. He wears a dark uniform trimmed in red for the occasion, and long sideburns, not for the occasion. It simply looks more serious, more dignified, and his wife told him that they make his jaw seem stronger.

The fleet is made up of brand new steamships: the frigates *Triunfo* and *Resolución*, which will meet up with the *Vencedora* in Montevideo, and then with the schooner *Virgen de Covadonga* near the mouth of the Rio de la Plata.

The builders of the *Virgen de Covadonga* would have been astonished to hear that she would be part of the armada. The admiralty had commissioned her to carry mail between Manila and Hong Kong, nothing fancy. But she was soon promoted because of the fine figure she cut and her smooth handling. After a few surgical procedures performed in the port of Buenos Aires – including a cannon graft – she is deemed fit to collect scientific data.

Simón Cristiano Claro is aboard the *Triunfo*. He, too, is astonished to find himself there, to have been swept along to the point of an actual voyage without ever having had either the desire or a great-great-grandfather with a penchant for globetrotting. Long ago, he had thought that life would give him clues to his true destiny, but those clues remained subtle, impenetrable: a pleasant childhood, military school to dispel boredom, the rank of lieutenant in exchange for mediocre grades, phases that always ended without a signpost of revelation. So he finds himself where he is put down, with no cocked hat, being judged by the women, hauling a case of sherry. Simón puts it down, stops on the deck, looks at Spain, which is still waking up. The sun is rising toward noon.

The order is given to cast off. They sail off in silence. The onlookers soon disperse. The illusion persists of a mere pleasure cruise and an imminent return. But they know better; they will play a great deal of whist, and there may be some danger. Because, really, they are showing the world that Spain still has ships, ships fitted with cannons.

The year is 1862.

So far no one is dead, no one is in love.

2

Diego Luna Sánchez Ortuño was a widower and too young to be one. He oversaw his land, dividing his time between his villa in Callao and his plantations in Lambayeque. The short trips involved in this effort kept him from getting bored. In the coach, he would imagine himself the owner of plains he caught glimpses of, he would put his affairs in order and calculate projected revenue. Then he would take a break to look at the mountain. He would knit his brow when he saw a condor, smile when he saw that there was already snow in the peaks. He liked winter, but couldn't say why. The cold clarified his thoughts. The white reminded him of his wife. The enamel of her teeth, the cotton of her underthings.

After a time, he began to tire of his journeys. He was already managing the fields he imagined he owned. Some of them were declining in profitability. He sold. Even rest had become tedious. He had seen the snow too many times, its comings and goings; and the condors could hardly be called acrobats. Their turns were too slow to make onlookers dizzy. They were desperately short on dives.

So he asked his son to join him.

In the coach, he held forth on the nature of the seeds sown: corn, rye, sorghum. He complained about the inefficiency of the labourers hired in the spring, natives and former slaves who arrived under the asiento. Discipline would have to be tightened.

The son learned fast, even making a few too many suggestions. He was just thirty years old, although almost bald, and his eagerness to take the torch was apparent. They inevitably wound up butting heads: the son criticized, the father scolded. You and the seasonal workers. You get too friendly with them. You whisper in their ear and even pat them on the shoulder. You have to keep your distance. Otherwise you'll end up doubling their salaries out of friendship.

You'll end up cutting their hours out of pure compassion. You'll end up going broke.

The lesson over, Diego withdrew into a deep silence. Out of habit he searched the sky for condors but found them only in his head. Insurmountably dark ideas circled, making him regret having left Spain, and then having never returned, and then everything else in equal measure: having lived in general and having eaten only a hard-boiled egg for breakfast, with no salt.

He reflected on his past, his index finger on his temple.

Hot days in Murcia, meeting his wife in front of the Cathedral Church of Saint Mary. She was leaving confession, feeling greatly relieved. Because this time she had thought herself beyond redemption. She had read a love story and spent a long time staring at a man's moustache. Hell had opened up beneath her feet, and it was so nice, burning, with scarlet lips, vermillion tongues, other unmentionable colours. The priest had been magnanimous. She could go in peace, on the condition that she return more often, because God loved her very much.

She fluttered down the steps to the square, feeling a weight lifted, redeemed for her weekly lapse in virtue, virginal once more. In her expiatory enthusiasm, she almost tripped. Diego caught her. Dishevelled, in the arms of a man, here we go again. She was thinking that she would have to go back up the stairs, get in line again, explain to the diamond-patterned profile in the half-light that grip was not the chief quality of women's shoes. Diego was thinking that his search was finally over, aside from, naturally, the search for more suitable accommodations to replace his bachelor's apartment. He could say goodbye to the unseemly places he would no longer have to haunt, friends he would no longer have to spend time with – new bosoms and new games, goodbye. She smelled like spice. He was thinking that the past no longer mattered, as long as she never found out about it, except for the matter of the inheritance from the grandfather, and a lineage that should not be kept quiet either.

He raised his eyes so that she wouldn't see them clouded with tears. At this time of day, the sun turned the cathedral bell tower pink, as if sculpted from coral. They were both moved at the same time, not something that happens every day. And in the months that followed, they were moved to the point that they decided to wed. At the Cathedral Church of Saint Mary, under the coral bell tower, before the priest, who was also moved.

Then came the flood of 1834. Without warning, the Segura jumped out of its bed and set off to find Diego in his sleep. It entered the house, climbed the stairs and lay down at his side. His wife was gone.

She liked to go down into the garden at night and fall asleep in the cool air, so the river may have carried her off like a kidnapped lover. Or perhaps she had drowned, like an illness that stops the heart without inducing a cough or laboured breathing, laying itself down on Ophelia without her stirring, aside from a shudder, a flutter. Or maybe she had run off before the water got there. The water was already up to Diego's waist. Half-asleep, he saved his daughter and his young son, both babies.

The sun rose on the flooded town, making it glisten. Bodies floated here and there, not many, just enough to bring grief to every neighbourhood. The coral bell tower, which was nice and dry, looked down over streets turned to rivers. Diego searched for his wife in vain, begged the priest: none of the parishioners knew, none of them wanted to know. When the pain is too great, most men take refuge at their mother's, disappear into the fields or board steamers. With no home or possessions, Diego left for Peru. He held his daughter with his right hand, his son under his left arm. He would have gone anywhere.

The son's voice chased the condors away.

Father, we're here. Be careful, it's muddy. The coachman slipped.

They took care with their boots. Once inside the hacienda, they took care with the marble floor. Diego and his son listened to the foreman's report – the son attentively, the father much less so. His wife was still on his mind: the flood, her disappearance. Diego was winning his battles against melancholy less often.

They went to visit the crops. The foreman explained that the workers were complaining of low wages. The son nodded, looked at his father who was lost in Spain, again. The dun horses had a hard time making their way through the marl and the ruts. Finally they arrived at the tract of land the seasonal workers were weeding. The son and the foreman dismounted and went to talk to a short, heavyset man, a descendant of the Incas, who represented the workers.

And then Diego saw her, the young woman, kneeling and pulling weeds. She was sweating; her black hair clung to her neck. The sun made the wet locks on her neck shine, like thick, dark veins filled with blood. She was an exact replica of his wife, an impossible copy, as though, when she disappeared, an unseen force had kept her imprint and carried it on the wind to this place across the ocean, an identical snowflake found in another part of the world. An exact reproduction with a jaw too weak to be an Inca's, the nose a little flat, down to the curves. Although the miracle hadn't gotten her chin quite right.

Bring her to my rooms, he said.

The heavyset man gripped his sickle; the foreman pushed him away. The son was surprised to hear his father, ordinarily so taciturn, speak in front of the men. The son came back toward him, had him repeat it, took offence at having heard right. Never before had anyone behaved this way, at least since Pizarro. Relations between management and labour were strained enough. They couldn't allow lucre, much less lust, to disturb the peace at the hacienda. Not lust, said the father. A sense. Perhaps a feeling.

And the son knew that his father loved a ghost.

The deed done, and in spite of her reticence, Diego made the woman promise to stay after the harvest. She was from Cuzco. Her hands smelled like potatoes. He would visit her often, perhaps marry her. She could loll about in a big canopy bed, a feather bed. She would have dresses and eat goose. But right now, he told her, I have to be off. We are invited to a reception in Callao, and my daughter is there alone. You know, I love her so much, although she says not enough, and I'm trying to pamper her. She's been sighing a little too much lately. Particularly since her brother has been coming with me on these trips. It's as though her mind is labouring over pyramids and labyrinths, and she wears herself out.

He added solemnly, Pity those lonely souls who reign over people who are imaginary.

He had read that in a newspaper quoting something like *Don Quixote.* He hadn't read *Don Quixote*, but his daughter had.

Diego Luna Sánchez Ortuño and his son left for Callao. The son looked out the window of the coach, not speaking, counting condors. At the bottom of the staircase, Diego had ordered the foreman to treat her better, to sneak her into the manor from time to time so she could sleep there, on the sly. He had called her by his late wife's name.

And the son knew that the manor was haunted.

María Montserrat Sánchez Ortuño wasn't as lonely as her father claimed. She was indeed awaiting his return in his apartments in Callao, but without impatience or anxiety. Elbows on her work table, she was reading a book on psychology. The term was still new at the time, or old enough to leave in its wake a multitude of names, thinkers and ideas she liked to lose herself in. Englishmen – Esdaile, Braid, Hamilton, whom she read in their mother tongue; Frenchmen – Liébault, Coué, Charcot, whom she read in their mother tongue; Germans – Herbart, Fechner, Bessel, whom she read, somewhat annoyed with herself, in translation.

People were saying that the Americans were studying this new science and were developing methods. In New York, they were discovering farther and farther reaches of the human mind. Darker, more pathological, so, ultimately, more fascinating. And she wouldn't have to learn another language to read the findings of their research – what a relief.

She remembered everything she read: the words, the typos, the semicolons. Her phenomenal memory meant that she could vaguely remember the flood and the coral pink bell tower. A long voyage by boat. But it also meant she could remember every encounter of her life. When she couldn't sleep at night, she thought back to someone, at random, and was astonished to find she had so many regrets.

Montse put aside her reading to look out the window. The ocean was calm and as yet empty. The sun struck her thick, wavy hair, unleashing the red; when sun hit her hair, it seemed to set it ablaze, glowing red, astonishing, even alarming. Under the burning sprigs hid the face of a bird, a tiny mouth, a receding chin. The nose was delicate, down to the nostrils, which, being a little too large, suggested a fiery temperament, or a past life as a Minotaur.

Another contrast: in the middle of the fire, there were two lakes in the form of shining eyes. Their depths gleamed as if harbouring pearls the size of the moon, Excalibur emerging from the depths, perhaps astigmatism. Curiosity, wonder and youthfulness were apparent in them. But people often misjudge their host, because Montse was already worried about being in her mid-thirties. The official old maid of Callao, she had never found love. Sometimes she looked back at her memories, but there was nothing there. To the point that she no longer looked. She had never found El Dorado, or Atlantis. It wasn't that Montse didn't know how to love or that she hadn't been loved. The problem was one of timing.

She loved; the object of her affection didn't realize it.

She was loved; she fled.

In the latter case, she often feigned distraction, even deafness. She ignored certain questions, as if they had never been asked. Do you love me? It's such a nice day. Will we see each other again? What do you think of the Murcia bell tower? Now she remembered their questions, and her evasive words. Sometimes she surprised herself by murmuring a clear answer, changing her answers, too late. The man was dead or married – in any event, far away as she lay in her bed. The verdict could not be appealed. I am one of those people who lives on a delay, Montse thought. On a time lag or in books, but never truly.

She was also beginning to get used to the idea of dying alone, without a hand to hold. She still had nice breasts, a nice smile. A small belly was blooming under her dress, made of the fat that would eventually settle there, creating the impression that she was a few months' pregnant, as if. Every morning she tightened her corset.

She went back to her reading. It said that the human mind contains all worlds except the one we live in. She was waiting for her father and her brother. She didn't feel as lonely as all that.

3

The men played a lot of cards aboard the *Triunfo*. They kept track of the days in wins and losses. To remember Tuesday, for instance, they thought of three aces and a lost snuffbox. Wednesday was remembered more fondly for the pair and the resulting small gold-plated chain, and then there was the return of the snuffbox on Thursday.

As luck would have it, some men grew rich in tobacco, and others grew rich in matches. They jealously guarded their possessions, using subterfuge to get what they were missing from a shipmate. They increasingly pulled fast ones, and lies became less scrupulous. There was an epidemic of dubious claims of seasickness to avoid playing, and then claims of miraculous cures.

On the advice of the captain, the sailors took to bartering, at least after he pointed out the rip in the royal sail that had to be repaired, if they were to do things by the book.

The next one who gets angry, he said, the next one who says he's sick …

Simón Cristiano Claro hadn't played much, preferring another way to keep track of the days. He had a good memory and a calendar in which he dispassionately noted the significant events of the day. This fact, which others mistakenly took for restraint, along with a certain facility with the written word, had quickly made him the ship's official scribe. The captain gave him orders to recopy, correspondence to embellish, a log to keep.

He wrote official reports, which were sent to Admiral Pinzón aboard the *Resolución*. Soon he was being congratulated on amusing turns of phrase. Communiqués went back and forth between ships, ultimately creating a short story of a crossing.

Seaman injured while mopping, barrel sent careening on account of a broken rope, discovery of a woman among the crew — thrown overboard.

Simón crossed out that last fabrication. It was too much, too funny to be plausible – after all, they weren't pirates or vaudeville players.

Because, to be honest, the days rarely brought more than three aces. His memory and his calendar brought nothing more to mind than an expanse of grey with some blue thrown in and, since the Brazilian coast had come into view, stretches of green and beige. But they were still sailing too far from shore to pick out any interesting details, and had been sailing too close to the high seas for too long for it to continue to make them dream. So they stayed the course, walking that thin line of ennui between the beautiful women in port and the giant octopus, a sort of blind spot of the voyage which, while offering hope of an imminent change of scenery, maintains a calming distance between the subject and object, a buffer zone typical of the all-inclusive holiday. No colonies of monkeys to the one side, no halcyon to the other – and no bathing beauties anywhere to be seen.

A few ports of call and accompanying shore leaves had given the crew a sneak peek of America and Simón new subjects for a chromatic study: the conjoined silhouettes of *Vencedora* and *Virgen de Covadonga*, the brown expanses of women's bodies – with green, blue or grey eyes. The latter expanses were mostly not suitable for telling, perpetuating the white expanse of the page. Simón found himself looking forward to Cape Horn which, for centuries, in addition to killing men, had offered inspiration for ships' logs. Beautiful scenes worthy of Victor Hugo: seagulls, the sea, death.

But they rounded the Horn without incident; it did little to defend its reputation as a graveyard of the sea. Waves licked the decks. To one side, in the distance, the sailors saw the bones of a ship smashed on a reef.

To quote Simón:

Two icebergs drifted together, glistening as they melted. They seemed to be holding each other's great icy hands underwater, turning slowly like two drunks waltzing.

In the masts, seagulls were taking a breather from the wind.

But men falling overboard, there were none.

So he had to settle for including humble anecdotes to spice up the report of the crossing. The captain didn't check anything – *approved, approved* – and then sent the reports to Admiral Pinzón on the *Resolucíon* or to the captains of the *Vencedora* and the *Virgen*. These ships then sent the *Triunfo* this same sort of report, containing similar misadventures with mops, rigging and castaways.

Simón wondered whether any of these episodes were true, or whether a particular one was false, tried to detect inspiration stowing away in the truth. Were they trying to entertain the other crews the way he was? They were probably having a bit of fun, too. Reality seemed to be crumbling around him as the weeks went by, and a false reality had replaced the routine gloom. Ghost ships, he thought, faded silhouettes lost among the waves and lies. Three companions that distance turns into strangers and that merely share the same ports.

But invention also has its boring bits: chamois cloth, rigging, stowaways, paint as faded as the beige wallpaper it was originally meant to hide – wallpaper formerly held in contempt that once again becomes intriguing, that people want to see again, its interest having been restored by having been forgotten. After all, isn't truth what relieves boredom?

❧

They docked at Valparaíso on April 18, 1863. Spain had recognized Chile's independence twenty-three years earlier. So there was no fuss, and no one was made to feel uncomfortable, other than having to get trussed up in full regalia. The appropriate hands were shaken. They visited, in order of protocol, the generals, financiers and aristocrats who requested it. They attended several receptions, where they met the president of Chile, José Joaquín Pérez, on a number of occasions.

He carried a gold-headed cane.

His hair was white and his face smooth.

He was also the president of the National Ballet.

One evening, over after-dinner drinks, Admiral Pinzón asked President Pérez about his dual role.

Presiding over the ballet must offer a change of pace, Pinzón said.

The entertaining part is being president of Chile, Pérez replied.

The visits went on for close to three months. Simón accompanied the captains and Admiral Pinzón as chronicler. He wrote a few lines about the wittier remarks and the turkey stuffed with apples.

To survive, he took walks during the day, left dinners early at night. He wandered the city, exploring the same streets over and over. The sun was invariably lukewarm. The wind, less lukewarm, swept down from the mountains and made him turn up the collar on his coat.

He observed and was observed.

And then, after a few weeks, no one noticed him anymore.

He took notes.

Valparaíso was barely above water. It was a city of half-tones, watered-down colours that seemed to hold the memory of a long time spent below the surface.

The people spoke in whispers. The music was played low. It seemed to come from the bottom of the sea and get lost among the squalls.

Ladies lazed along the squares and docks. Having forgotten a mantilla after mass, they let their thick hair blow in the breeze; it was soon damp from the sea spray and turned to seaweed.

In the shops, they were received by people who looked like ghosts. They were too mild, too calm. It was as if the entire city knew it was condemned to return to the waves. They hypnotized anyone who watched them. The soul became one with them, the body begged to be thrown into them. The eye could make out all sorts of shapes in the uniform wash and the even swell. The foam became clouds: a giraffe, an astrolabe, someone. The face of Julius Caesar followed by a more familiar nose.

Is it really you after all these years? You're coming back to me, here, in Valparaíso?

So it was hard to blame the locals for being so contemplative. It was as if they wanted to melt into the arms of a wave, the next one, that one, the one after that. The sailors had never seen such dangerous seas. Not even rounding Cape Horn.

There was no fault to be found with Chile, no one to blame. Both the speeches and the women were beyond reproach. Both had faint flattery for Spain and its men. The feeling was mutual.

July came and, under the same sun, with the same wind, Admiral Pinzón gave the order to cast off. Some of the crew were short on enthusiasm; others feigned it better. Everyone had grown weary of Valparaíso, of course, but they had grown used to the weariness. It had turned into a bit of happiness that they would use to fill their old age, spent on the balcony watching the shadows move and the neighbour whose husband travels.

So they left the city and its pastels. Along with the dignitaries, a few women came to say goodbye to a few men. They tossed handkerchiefs. They made each other no promises. Slowly, the houses rose up in tiers on the hillsides. The docks emptied. And the sea met the horizon, like a curtain falling on the set, like an eyelid on a dream.

4

The ships sailed on to Peru to continue (lest we forget) the great scientific expedition. Simón had indeed collected two or three leaves and as many flowers in the streets. He kept them between pages in a scrapbook. He looked at them when he needed inspiration. They didn't offer any.

On the ships they enjoyed a few days of an all-inclusive holiday. Then they spotted Callao shrouded in fog. They had time to watch the fog dissipate, revealing the first coastal battery, then a stately building surrounded by beautiful statues, which was its city hall; as a final touch, the sun sparkled on the waters in the port. The ships approached still-empty piers. The buildings had few windows. People flocked to them to watch the fleet come in. The sea offered up so few ships.

They threw out the rigging. They had to wait a few minutes before anyone appeared to tie them to the bollards and then a few minutes more before they could disembark in dignity. The Peruvians had known a scientific expedition was coming, of course; a reception had been planned. But the fleet was early or, in any case, more than on time – Spanish ships braved the seas too well. It was unexpected.

Pinzón shook the hands that were held out to him, the hand of a priest, a stranger, a mayor. All more firmly than in Chile. Because nothing had been made official between Spain and Peru; nothing had been recognized. The independence of 1821 remained a point of contention. For one of the nations, the matter had been settled forty-two years earlier; for the other, there had never been a matter at all. In fact, they wouldn't discuss it.

The Spaniards nonetheless asked where Juan Antonio Pezet was. They were told that the new president was running late, detained at the bedside of the former president who was not quite done dying, but that he would come from Lima. He was on his way. No doubt he would be at the reception being held the next day, along with the generals. Will you come?

Yes, we'll come, Pinzón replied.

They embraced. There were a further three minutes of trumpets and bassoons. Then one party returned to the ships, the other to Callao.

Simón had to accompany Admiral Pinzón that evening.

Make sure you record any Peruvian witticisms and the Peruvian turkey stuffed with apples. You can describe Pezet and the others, Peruvians I think. Don't forget my scathing comebacks, maybe an exotic dish or two.

It will delight Isabelle later on, the food in particular.

Despite this encouragement, Simón had to search the mirror for motivation. For History, no; for country, better – but a century from now, who would care about a handful of descriptions of high society, the sheen of a moustache, the cut of a corset? Finally he fell back on the same motivation that always worked. Seeing reflected in women's eyes that his long journey inspired awe – yes, that's it, off we go.

Simón's beard and hair had seen better days. His weariness showed in his uniform: a patch of dust at the elbow, a button missing from the collar. The sea and Valparaíso had dulled his interest in his appearance. It was as if he had returned from a long time spent lost at sea and was not expecting much of himself or the food that was served. Anything would be better than coconuts or surrendering to the waves.

They approached city hall. The night was still warm. It was filled with chirping and the lapping of waves caught between docks and hulls. Dew was settling over them as they walked, glazing the medals and épaulettes.

They went in.

Life was noisier inside. Less pleasant too. It was filled with men. The new arrivals were announced. The word *admiral* was said loudly, the word *Spain* as well. There were looks and nods of heads. One could sense a bit of underlying impertinence. Then the conversations interrupted by Pinzón's arrival resumed with new vigour: laughter, rude remarks, hypocrisy. Simón looked on.

A large table filled half the room; place settings filled half the table. Simón didn't recognize half the guests. The men sported long useless swords and revolvers; the women wore equally long dresses – but they were pretty, almost useful – and carried fans.

A bit disoriented, Simón followed Pinzón as he zigzagged between groups, greeting such-and-such a diplomat as he passed, masking a forgotten name with a compliment or kisses to the hands of wives unknown.

They reached the mayor, bowing and scraping. You're here at last. People were growing impatient, of course, you know, you're the main attraction; you're the evening's high point. The Spaniards were introduced to other important dignitaries.

These included a Brit, who had come to observe, and Manuel Ignacio de Vivanco, a general. He was a Peruvian with a handlebar moustache. He was on trend.

The introductions kept coming. The men weren't very well entertained – they even missed Chile a little. The mayor's arm drew great swirls in the air, people came, the mayor spoke, four words were exchanged before they were bid a fine evening. The merry-go-round started up again, they were bid a good time.

To keep good form, they circulated a little, and the mayor ushered Pinzón over to a group of guests. Oh, ah, delighted. They inquired politely after Madrid. Pinzón returned the courtesy. He knew his capitals.

He even discussed Washington with an American commodore. The commodore was all too willing. Battles were being waged in his country. Plenty of blood spilled, men turned to hamburger by

Gatlings. A fine state of affairs. Imagine your homeland, dear Pinzón, torn apart by a civil war. Imagine killing your cousin and your platoon-mate raping his niece. And all over ideas. Ideas! A bit of cotton, too. Can you imagine?

The commodore was likeable and knew how to tell stories about his country. He had the name of a cowboy: John Rodgers.

President Pezet was keeping the guests waiting. He might arrive after dinner, in time for the play. He enjoyed the theatre and even more so the actress playing Juanita. Until then, they would wait, shake a few more hands. In his mind, Simón had already written a thousand passages of his report. In fact, he had it practically all sewn up. Because the action kept repeating itself: three or four bits of wordplay in rotation, the announcement of a piece of news about the port of Cadix and the fleet's next destination. It was San Francisco.

A nice city, said John Rodgers. A young city. A city of the future. There's gold. You'll like it, except for the Chinese – it's the West.

The evening seemed to run in a loop. A sort of interminable nursery rhyme that only sleep or exile to an inner world can save you from. The walls of that sleep or inner world would have to be thick, preferably soundproof. Stupidity carries.

Simón saw a man with a moustache come in, followed by a much younger man who was balding. They headed toward him. Behind them was a woman. He saw her hair out of the corner of his eye. She was not wearing a mantilla – she never did. The wives in her path stared at her. Insolence, immodesty! I mean, really. Would you ever see such a thing in Lima?

Simón didn't attach any importance to this lack of decorum. In any case, it seemed to him that the only thing that could contain the flaming head of abundant hair would be an iron helmet. It would have reduced mere threads to ashes.

Introductions were once again summary. The father and son were delighted to meet Admiral Pinzón and indifferent to meet Simón. The daughter's face suggested the opposite. She had the small face of a bird in a nest of hair. Simón puffed out his chest, gripped his sword, steeled his eyes. She held out her hand to him.

She was mild in manner, reminding him of the night that was going on, outside, without the men.

Simón Cristiano Claro, he said.

Montse, she said.

It didn't end there.

Although that's how it may have appeared. Because they each had to go bow and scrape elsewhere. After that Simón could catch only glimpses of Montse. She slid between two shadows, sometimes passing near him. He felt her presence constantly, without really wanting to. She was behind him, to his left, to his right, slipping too far away, coming back too close. He sensed her, caught hints of her, a homing mechanism that was rather intoxicating, lending credence to the idea of a sixth sense, explained perhaps by an unusually wide field of vision or the complex matter of pheromones, which was only enhanced by the various types of mirrors placed here, there and everywhere: a vanity mirror between the windows, a trumeau mirror near the hearth, and even — such a lovely convenience — a rear-view mirror on the ceiling.

Montse was looking at the uniform, particularly the pants, particularly the back of the pants, the way they fell, the pleats, a certain roundedness. Simón didn't see her watching him. She found him a bit dishevelled, too dusty at the elbows. She studied his face again. The beard would need some tending. Simón was talking to the American. He was from Boston. He liked his city. The sea, a bay, foreigners: sort of the mirror image of San Francisco, with a touch of elegance to boot.

Dinner was announced. As custom would have it, the women were seated first, then the men, then the officers, and finally the senior ranks.

His turn came, and Simón went to sit at the rounded end of the table. He was trying to sit as far from any guests as possible. Distance helps with exile. He wanted to avoid talking so he could dream. Maybe he would manage to write a bit more in his head.

But Montse, who was already seated, waved him over. They were separated by a few chairs, and as many carafes and knives. You're so far away, come here, come over. She pointed to an empty seat next to her. She wasn't terribly discreet: an obvious look, her hand flapping. But her voice remained calm, resting on silences that she embellished with smiles.

It would have been boorish to ignore her. Simón complied, thinking the invitation a little odd. Had someone told her about him? She was behaving as if they knew each other: a cousin he had played with under the willow tree, a special friend whose love letters had been slipped under the door long ago. It was like a reunion after a long separation, such ridiculous moments. Except, of course, when they are one's own. Then it is more like magic – how marvellous the world is, how could I have forgotten? Poetry took on new meaning, the heart became more than just an organ, ah, yes. Let us sing.

Still, Simón kept a modicum of control. He took his seat near Montse, without running or knocking over the vases of daffodils with his sword. Immediately there were questions about the menu.

Have you ever tried this dish?

What do you think of the sherry?

Simón recognized nothing.

Besides, it had been ages since he had talked to a woman. He wondered what he should say, after the small talk. Perhaps more small talk.

The table filled up without him noticing. The American was seated across from him. Ashamed of his culinary ignorance, Simón looked for a way out. John Rodgers just happened to pick up their conversation where they had left off. He talked about Boston some more. Beautiful city, nice port, cradle of the revolution. Montse was still looking at the menu. There would be eight courses.

John Rodgers talked of tea thrown overboard, then of war, of History. Simón was perplexed for a moment; he found the thread leading from tea to war a bit tenuous. America, my good man, America! It blazes new trails and conquers destiny on its own terms. It is awe-inspiring. It is the future.

It was hard to know what to say next.

When John Rodgers paused in extolling the virtues of his country, Montse asked Simón what he thought of the forthcoming dessert, of the appetizer they'd just finished, and then of each of the eight courses, which she rearranged all the same; finally, what did he prefer to drink? Simón answered hastily. To drink with dessert? Probably coffee.

Montse wouldn't relent. She boldly asked indiscreet questions. She spoke of her travels, her fears, of how important she considered reading. Of her steadfast efforts in the little essays she wrote.

She even asked him for advice about studies she was thinking of pursuing in Lima. Simón answered clearly and concisely, then turned the conversation back to John Rodgers, who wouldn't let up. Tea, revolution, George Washington chopping down a cherry tree. Without realizing it, he was doing the very thing that fascinates women: he listened, guided, advised, and most of all, he didn't push. But with each new snippet of conversation, Simón felt his centre of interest move from the American to the feminine. Tired of Boston, the port and the revolution, he began to appreciate Lima and psychology. In any case, John Rodgers' moustache was losing its mystery – grey hairs, black hairs, crumbs. He was more interested in Montse's delicate hands. She did everything patiently: putting down a fork, raising a glass, smoothing an invisible fold in the tablecloth to make it disappear – it was as if she were tending to a scar or, how would you describe it, divinely reshaping a sculpture in relief, eroding a chain of snow-topped mountains until flat.

The *coup de grâce* was delivered. The meal was over, and the guests withdrew to the drawing room or the boudoir. John Rodgers was smoking with the mayor and the admiral, who wanted to talk about John Rodgers Senior, a celebrity. Montse pulled Simón over to the hearth. Behind her, the heavy drapes of a tall window blended with the fabric of her dress, increasing its volume threefold. Moments earlier, Montse had been talking about the possibility of an apartment in Lima, spending her time studying, perhaps receiving minds, great minds, or at least average minds, the puny ones having all settled here anyway. And then, more generally, of being uprooted, of people who abandon their birthplace, hearts that follow other hearts. I would have a hard time leaving, said Montse, my family, you know. Simón replied that an interesting posting could make him want to relocate. Or a woman, yes, love. Yes, quite honestly, those were the only things that could tear him away from Spain. A greater glory or a greater love. Than Spain.

Silence had returned, but Montse's smiles hadn't. She seemed pensive now that they were revealing a bit more to one other.

A few minutes went by. The glowing embers of the conversation that Simón had had with the American endured among the smokers: he could hear an aside about New York, a digression about herbal tea. And Montse returned to her thoughts.

I think it's interesting what you suggested, she said, about women. About women?

Yes, about a woman who could make you stay or go.

Things were moving fast. Or she was teasing. Had he made that much headway with Montse? They barely knew each another.

But Montse was already in her thirties. Time was gnawing at her face, pinching the corners of her mouth, squeezing her neck. The corners of her eyes were growing puffy, and small roots appeared to be spreading toward the temples. Was it possible that this haste, this sincerity … From that point on, Simón saw nothing more of the reception, of America, of Admiral Pinzón who, in the company of the mayor, was yawning. This women was offering herself to him, maybe. Their talk became more intense, more wild. Yes, she repeated, I would have a hard time leaving Callao.

And yet you weren't born there, Simón said.

But it's where I learned everything I know, she replied.

She argued that you belong to the place that has the most memories for you.

But the number of memories says nothing about their power, Simón said. Sometimes a place can mark you with just one memory. But it haunts you forever. You never leave that place. You stay there forever.

Can you tell me what place possesses you so? she asked.

I have too many ghosts inside me, he answered.

Simón was using mystery now. He was manoeuvring, employing strategy. And it also had a bit of truth – to the extent that he considered others' stories his own: Boston, Murcia, the dramas and tragedies that mark a life.

They would not stay this inspired for long. They would go on to discuss theatre, literature and music. A little politics. Nothing terribly substantial.

But the underlying themes of distance, hearts and great passions kept reappearing. For example, the topic of European Romanticism afforded Montse an opinion cautioning against the follies that love demands.

The Chevalier des Grieux can claim to have tried everything, to have given in to his inclination to the point of being horizontal.

Montse admired him. She regretted never having put her heart on the line. She explained, of course with more grace, that all this time she had placed too much value on time, and she had never been able to give it to others. She guarded it jealously for herself. She hated the idea of having wasted time, should love fail. Putting off her reading, her work, her life, for a love that would end up, in all likelihood, fading.

An hour gained, happiness lost, Simón preached.

She thought his words sentimental. And perhaps rightly so.

Because she was getting old enough to feel the emptiness of days not shared. They disappear. Who has seen them with you? Who can vouch for what you have experienced? No one, right?

Simón Cristiano Claro and Montse Sánchez Ortuño were now completely absorbed in each another. She was studying one of his scars, a fine pink line hidden in his right eyebrow. He was discovering a colony of crow's feet near her eyelid, a wrinkle like a reed under her lip. They were both trying to keep the conversation going. When they allowed themselves silence, it was to think of what to say next, and then later on, and then later on still, to keep the conversation from ending. They were planning four or five moves ahead, thinking back to chess matches they had won. She finally talked about her most recent reading. She had been holding the topic in reserve for a while, and it was the only thing that came to mind.

Our minds contain all possible worlds, she said, except the one we live in.

Then she added, sadly, This one isn't inside us, can't be inside us, it's ... outside.

Simón was more perplexed than he had been with the American and the jettisoning of tea bags. He searched for an illuminating response, dismissed three stupid ones. Finally he managed to summon a thought.

I think that all the worlds inside us make up this one.

Montse smiled; Simón exhaled. She liked his views, which were so different from everyone else's, and his ideas, which weren't hackneyed. At least when he wasn't talking about clocks and happiness. And then there were his sea-weary eyes, a little dull from a distance, and yet bright from having spent months absorbing the sun reflecting off the sails. She saw herself in them. Particularly in the weariness, truth be told.

But Simón didn't realize he had done so well. Little by little, Montse was growing more distant. Sometimes she looked over at the American or grew quiet to listen to a nearby discussion about lace. Maybe it was part of her game. Now he was the one asking questions. She seemed groggy from having given too much, hesitant to advance any more. Her retreat stirred Simón's passions. Desire clouded his head, took over his body. It reached dizzying heights and unanticipated depths. And then a fragrance enveloped him: spices, soft light marked by one or two storm clouds, electric. His nostrils quivered from breathing too fast.

And her gestures were part of what bewitched him. Montse twirled a finger in her hair. Her skin didn't burn and Simón was astonished – a fascination that was interrupted only by the butler's announcement. The play, ladies, gentlemen, lovebirds.

⁊✦

Juanita was the only thing on the mad Alessandro's mind. Also on the mind of President Pezet, who appeared the moment the curtain went up. Neither had professed his love to the beauty, and now they were consumed with regret.

Admiral Pinzón had been seated to Pezet's left. They exchanged brief greetings, complimented outfits and beards and thanked each other for being there. Pinzón yawned again, infecting Pezet, who in turn contaminated the mayor before the curtain rose, revealing what looked like a red throat at the back of which dangled the uvula of a cardboard chandelier. This particular yawn would last an hour, multiplying those of the hosts. Simón and Montse were side by side, as if wrapped in a cocoon of their mingling scents. But they didn't touch each other. The tip of a nail occasionally reached the vicinity of Simón's elbow, the end of a hair Montse's wrist. It became impossible to tell whose finger was headed where. But every gesture ran aground, went unseen, stayed a secret that each of them knew the half of.

They did manage, just once, to bring the two ends of their desire together. There was an amusing moment in the play. Juanita had tricked Alessandro, a rabbit in a cupboard, a case of mistaken identity. Montse and Simón turned toward each other, simultaneously, spontaneously. They shared a laugh.

It occurred to Simón that he had not been lying earlier when he said that a woman could, you know.

The curtain fell. Bravo, encore, a further encore for Pezet. After all, he couldn't talk to Juanita, who was too beautiful, a gypsy at heart, enigmatic even.

She went from town to town performing. Pezet followed her whenever he could. And when he couldn't tear himself away – from a cabinet meeting or a brothel – he dreamed of her. He would play the role of Alessandro. But not the character from the play – Alessandro the actor, who went everywhere she did and was on stage with her every night.

There was a scene where he kissed her arm. Pezet played it back in his mind, at a leisurely pace, repeating it until it was absolute perfection. The wrist held tenderly, lips placed near the elbow, the slightest caress of the tongue, a retreat paired with a passionate look – and release. Exit. He didn't look back.

Pezet had to leave. Duty called.

He and Pinzón finally addressed each other again. More compliments were exchanged. One was repeated: it was a top-quality sword belt. The others would stay for a Chartreuse.

Except Montse, who was tired.

It was indeed late.

An honourable gentleman was duty bound to see her home. The darkness of the streets of Callao could not be underestimated. So Simón, who was a charitable soul, excused himself with Pinzón. His presence was no longer required; he had gathered everything needed to impress Isabelle, plenty of food and hairdos. And then there was the irrepressible desire to walk, the sense of duty.

A lady to see home? Pinzón asked.

Yes, that too, Admiral, Simón said.

He took his leave. In any event, Pinzón was not inspired by the digestif and hadn't worked out a witty remark. And one must not keep ladies waiting. But are you sure that you have enough faces and anecdotes? Yes, Admiral, and of course the nuances of the tomato sauce.

They left the reception. It was drizzling over Callao, a mist that turned the air velvet, making everything seem more distant. Passersby and coaches appeared suddenly and disappeared prematurely.

The faint droplets didn't soak through clothes, were no threat to socks. But the ladies, and their hairdos, imagine. So umbrellas were offered to those walking. A servant drew them from a large wicker basket and held them out to guests. The basket looked like a Vietnamese hat, upside down of course; as for the servant, he looked like Montezuma dressed by a good tailor. Simón took an umbrella, just in case. Montse was certainly a lady.

They went out into the night. It was as if the sky were reclining on a bed of embers. No, Simón explained, it's the water in the harbour, over there, gleaming. Oh, pardon me, I'm near-sighted, Montse confessed. The water, she murmured again. It glistened, reflecting the ships' lanterns, offering up little stars, faint and fleeting, that melted with the slightest ripples.

It also created, Simón mused, the illusion of a large pool filled with small coins. Then one just had to think of the wishes they represented – deep, lost, unhappy – and that might be competing with one another. Coins of the same value cancelled each other out; some people tossed in more than one to improve their chances. Hope was essentially mathematical, when you got right down to it. And the most valuable coin would probably win.

Not to mention the gold plate the shameless moon contributed. When one is that fortunate, good taste dictates wanting nothing more.

Simón and Montse were drawn by the light that wound its way between the hulls of the ships in the port. It was romantic. The water's edge always was, the charm of docks often was. They had each read Des Grieux twice, four times between them, which ends up giving one ideas. And one of these was to linger over the walk home. And they could find no better way than to head in the wrong direction.

Simón opened the umbrella. Too large for a single person, it was made for two. The people from the reception knew high society only too well. They were polite, they saw their wives home, if not a damsel in distress.

Montse huddled under the umbrella more than circumstances required. Its circumference should have allowed for more distance between them. And Montse normally didn't mind the rain in her hair – it was frizzy anyway. But right now, I mean, honestly, kinks, coils, the horror, so no. Let me take shelter near you, under your arm.

Simón began to smell the fragrance of spices near him, and the heat of the summer excited his thoughts. They were walking along the water's edge. To be considerate, Simón walked closest to the water. Montse huddled up, and then huddled up some more – I'm a bit cold – curling up against Simón as if fearing a danger. He was afraid she would push him in.

They looked everywhere and, when they could find no more wishes or lanterns to stare at, they stared mainly at their feet. But a passion for laces is hard to sustain, so Simón, feeling reckless, finally took the chance of gazing at Montse.

Her eyes looked like the tranquil waters of the port the rain fell on: dark, satiny, with barely perceptible sparkles like mosquitoes skimming the surface of a lake and dropping into it, having spent themselves in their acrobatics. It was actually the water of Callao and the evening's drizzle in her eyes. Montse was very much of this place. She blended into her surroundings, or vice versa, an admirable thing that made her whole, and simple, and sound, because she didn't resist the world, like the rest of us, crazy people that we are.

They had barely spoken since opening the umbrella. Is that okay, yes, thank you, the umbrella is too small, my hair, come closer. Once tucked into the silence, it was hard to break it. Words had seemed much less fraught with meaning in the din of the gala. Here, they filled the head and, perhaps, the heart.

Finally they arrived in front of Diego Luna Sánchez Ortuño's house. The walk home had seemed short, in spite of the lengths they had gone to to try to make it longer: small steps, stops on account of great exhaustion or the sore foot she feigned.

My, Montse said, we talked a great deal.

She hung back from the doorway, as if she didn't want to go inside.

Yes, Simón said, maybe a little too much.

Do you think? she said.

She waited expectantly, maintaining a secret, fragile balance, where nothing moved but where the slightest breath could have raised a storm. Her face strained forward. Her lips were jutting out from her face, her eyes became showers. She couldn't hold on for long.

In the face of the evidence, all Simón knew how to do was to run away. He preferred the comfort of doubt. He had drifted along this way for years, not knowing what he wanted, not taking what was offered to him. At least his dignity remained intact, along with the illusion of never having made a mistake.

All he could think to say was, Will I see you again?

Montse smiled, perhaps because he looked foolish or awkward at the very moment she had stopped being so, after so many failed attempts, when all she was asking for was a little shared courage.

Well, she said, my father leaves tomorrow for Lambayeque. But I'm staying here.

The fleet leaves tomorrow for San Francisco, Simón said. And I'm going with it.

She stopped smiling. He looked at her, apologizing with his eyebrows. I've ruined everything, he said to himself; I sabotaged our desire. When will I learn how to connect?

Then she pulled him inside. He barely had time to close the umbrella. She grabbed his wrist with a warm hand, even warmer than he had expected it to be, and softer, even softer than the white tablecloth she had smoothed so many times at dinner. He noticed that her nails had no lunulae.

Now they were in the vestibule. Facing one another. The persistent drizzle and the detours had rendered Montse's dress transparent around her ankles and her arms. Simón briefly regretted using the umbrella, while she looked for something on a small pedestal table.

The maid was frozen in the hallway, confused, as was the butler in the stairway. A man had come in the house. It wasn't the master, or his son. It was bound to happen someday, with Mademoiselle, who was too often buried in her books not to take leave of her senses.

You'll write me, Montse said. You know how to write. Letters.

Yes, letters, Simón repeated.

She took a gold pen from a writing case. This is for you, she said. Just for me. It seemed like a mixed message. For you, oh yes, for me, Simón said. For the letters I'm going to write you. It's beautiful, are you sure that ... One minute, just a moment, she whispered to the servants, my dear friends. The butler looked, descended a step, waited. The maid came closer, curious.

Simón stared at Montse. She held his hand tight, leaving white impressions that faded as soon as the blood returned. There was a bit of jungle in her eyes. Simón didn't know what to read in their darkness: anger or passion, a blend of desire and disappointment. Near-sightedness.

The butler finally stepped forward to admonish Montse, to remind her that the master would not approve; they didn't want a diplomatic incident.

Simón turned on his heel and left.

Montse stepped back out on the doorstep, waiting deep in her soul, under the ashes of renunciation for him to come back. But he didn't look back. Around him, the night was expanding, spreading like an ink stain, with him as the source. When he opened the umbrella and rested it on his shoulder, it looked as though an octopus had grabbed him and swallowed him.

❧

The idea of letters was a little mad. But some women pine. And they accept the growing foolishness of certain men – the outbursts, the insistence, the billet-doux delivered daily – and they wind up longing for them.

The next day, the father and son left for Lambayeque; you should have stayed for a Chartreuse last night, dear daughter. Pinzón told some good ones, excellent ones, to say nothing of the president of Chile.

The fleet headed to San Francisco.

No one came to the docks to say goodbye.

Simón rolled the gold pen between his fingers. Something remained of Montse's hand and transferred from the object to his skin, then to his head, which was dreaming. He didn't write; instead he imagined caresses given, received, repeated – out of respect, he went no further than the small of the back.

Montse was sitting at her table in front of the window, a book open in front of her. She wasn't reading. She was watching the world outside her mind, the one she so often fled. And the sea became the sea again, offering up no more ships.

5

Diego Luna Sánchez Ortuño once again surveyed his imaginary holdings, the mountains and the condors. Respectively, they were more profitable, all the snow had melted, they had not – mad hope – invented a new way to fly. He and his son were arguing over crop management again. Then, revisiting the previous evening's ball, they reconciled. They laughed at the mayor and the Spaniards; in spite of their notorious indifference, the Spaniards had been fairly civilized. One day they would all get along famously, who knows, maybe even sending ambassadors and exchanging official visits that – after a few zamacueca and fandango demonstrations reciprocally tolerated – would blossom into joint ventures.

Also, since the morning, Montse had been smiling a bit rapturously. She was even humming classical airs, an arietta by Nasolini. Diego thought he recognized his late wife in the tone of the voice singing – nearly in tune, but then consistently hitting the wrong note at the end of the verse or at the beginning of the phrase, sending emotion into a skid, ruining the rest. He politely brought up the idea of singing lessons, just to polish things up of course, and then questioned her directly about the reason for the solo, because the maid was trying to look busy and the butler was offering up emergencies as a pretext.

She thought her work was going rather well.

Was that all?

Well, yes, the evening had been fun. Pleasant encounters, charming people.

Charming? Her brother was surprised.

A playwright, an impresario? But he had to leave. The coach had been brought around. The horses were cold and stamping in the courtyard. We'll talk about this when I get back, Diego had said. It was what a father should say, he thought, to make sure he looked like a busy man without shirking his duty to stay informed. But afterward, later. Once the dispute with the workers in Lambayeque was settled, then he would take up the matter of her new flame.

Flames. At first Diego could see only the flames that rose above the manor, a great morphing cauliflower, its darkness eating away at the day. The mountains and condors were to be expected, as was the quarrel between father and son, but this smoke was disconcerting.

Approaching the hacienda, they realized that what was burning was a shed for ploughshares and ploughs. No one was trying to put out the blaze. They picked up their pace to warn or blame the plantation men, as circumstances required.

Father and son descended from the coach. The doors to the manor were wide open, but still they couldn't see inside: the sun and the shadows were both too intense. They climbed the steps and were surprised that they couldn't make things out any better once they were on the threshold; there was only darkness, and mystery. The silence was broken by the distant crackle of flames.

The entrance hall: here again it took some time to work out what was right before their eyes. It was like a woman who changes her hairstyle, a man who shaves his moustache – didn't you notice? The father and son's nerves were stretched taut from the suspense. Why the open door? Why the fire? There was something to these details, wasn't there? The brain can be lazy, and, shaken from routine, it takes some effort to rouse emotion again. Nerve endings have to be dusted off.

They risked about eight watchful steps. Their eyes were adjusting to the darkness: the lights were growing less pink and the darkness less thick. A darker mass lay to the right, like a big, moist, humped mushroom that had grown in the cool air.

It was the body of the foreman on top of the body of a servant, their skulls crushed from different angles, their bodies forming the

X on a treasure map, or the symbol of their death, the letter normally drawn on the eyelids to make things explicit, although not really necessary outside of the cartoon world. Crepes lay scattered around them, having fallen from a silver tray, which, lying between their heads, were the finishing touches on a sort of Ottoman or papal coat of arms.

They're dead, the son said, prodding them with a foot. We should pinch their nostrils. We should get out the smelling salts, ventured the father. The blood spreading on the marble formed a sort of upside-down tree, a liquid trunk that flowed into larger branches, then into diffuse foliage and roots that were still slowly growing. The soaked crepes looked like the coral moons of Symbolist painters. Let's go upstairs instead, Diego suggested.

They took great care with their boots.

They looked around the second floor. The son had a revolver in his hand, something he had never used. They suspected a raid by bandits, deep down feared the pishtaco, but there were no more bodies lying around to stumble over or terrorize them. Nothing appeared, cried out for help or lay in the wardrobes or behind doors. The order made them worry even more. They found themselves hoping they would discover a massacre, a drama that would have had the virtue of being plausible, to support a theory or at least to reassure them that what they were seeing was real. They even opened a cedar chest in the master bedroom. It was filled with clean linens and blankets. Disappointment.

They went back down to the entrance hall. The tree had grown.

Now more intrigued than worried, Diego and his son wanted to go back to the coach and drive around the fields. Through the manor's open door, in the sun, they saw the seasonal workers waiting for them by the coach.

They had the coachman. They looked angry.

Diego and his son decided resistance was futile. They would have to negotiate, give them a raise, build new bunks in the barracks, whatever. They stepped out onto the landing. The son was still holding the revolver, but he didn't have the nerve to fire. The rebels were armed with three or four guns, in addition to spades and rakes, but they were nonetheless worried about Diego's revolver. There were shouts, orders, threats made to the coachman, which weighed little in the balance. Diego threw the weapon into the flowerbed, amid the azaleas.

The Inca was the leader of the rebels. He gripped a machete in his right hand. The wife Diego had been reunited with was behind him.

It took some time to figure out what the problem was. The crowd dispersed, and the Inca said in a voice tinged with Quechuan inflections that the woman was his, and that his honour, his people, love, when you came right down to it – because it had reached that point – could not be violated. He stuttered with rage.

Understanding that a raise would not do the trick, Diego started to apologize. Had he known, had he been told. Someone should have said something. It was the foreman, the Inca fumed, who had advised him to keep quiet, to avoid everyone getting fired, to avoid making the master angry. Oh no, someone should have said something, of course. We would have listened, of course.

They grabbed the father and the son. They forced them to kneel surrounded by the workers. It was too late for talking, but not for spitting, which the Inca's wife did a great deal of. In Diego's face – have you seen this? – on Diego's hands – never, even in Cuzco where she came from, had they seen such a bastard. She slapped him. Her hands smelled of potatoes.

Diego closed his eyes, on account of the spitting, and then opened them again to look. Aside from the chin, she definitely looked like his late wife; and so it was as if it were his late wife now showering him in contempt. It seemed to him the appropriate punishment for having abandoned her in Segura, for having left their life, their house, everything they had dreamed of together.

To make amends, in his thoughts he often brought flowers to her grave. But does a thought count? It was too easy, too effortless, it took no energy and, while a thought can weigh on you, everyone thinks it's light. She probably would have wanted him to suffer a grief that is metabolized in sweat not in tears, and to try to restore their home. And that her children would come to see her, most of all. Murmuring a little prayer in front of the grave – Mama, I hope you are really where you are, look at my doll Camilla – things that soothe the conscience. But no, Diego had left death to be death, and nothing more.

His heart became her coffin.

The son, kneeling behind his father, didn't cry, didn't speak. He was thinking about what fools men could be when it came to women, and when it came to men for that matter, getting even more irritated since his position, kneeling on the pebbles, was uncomfortable. He thought of his sister, basically solitary, virtually cloistered, who had perhaps understood. You shouldn't play; you should bow out of the dance. Real life is peace and deep thoughts. He wanted to see her again so that she could tell him about books. He had never talked about psychology with her. From now on, he would take an interest.

Diego's skin was starting to go pruney from the spit. The other women joined the Inca's wife in showering him in contempt. The Inca decided that that was enough fun and games and that vengeance would now be his. There was no speech, no torture, really. The act was swift, performed by a man accustomed to cattle and fowl. He yanked Diego's pants down and took hold of his penis. He cut it off with his machete. Diego crumpled in the dust, falling slowly to one side, like a horseman hit by a bullet and sliding from his saddle. He moaned a little.

The Inca held the penis up for the stunned crowd; there was a smattering of polite cries, lacking real enthusiasm. What they had really wanted was a raise. The woman Diego and the Inca were fighting over earned a few more ululations and that was all. Silence settled on the scene. The father lost consciousness. The son was dumbstruck, looking at the organ that was at the origin of his life. The Inca was still holding it high, his arm outstretched. Blood trickled down his wrist, red ivy painting his skin, dripping down toward his elbow. He noticed the son's fascination and approached him. He forced him to open his mouth. He inserted the penis and made him chew.

Finish him off, the Inca finally said.

He pointed to Diego, who was barely conscious.

The crowd protested: was that strictly necessary? It was, now that hatred was running so high; otherwise it would get back to Callao, and there would be a scandal and retaliation. Diego protested in a weak voice.

There would be a scandal and retaliation anyway.

You still have balls, the Inca joked. Then he hit him, joking less.

In spite of everything, Diego kept talking while a man with a gun approached him. He wanted to change strategies and buy his life. He felt that he had been punished enough, thank you very much. His wife could forgive him. He patted the inside pocket of his frock coat, looked for the gold pen he normally carried with him, a beautiful object he could barter with. But it wasn't there. He thought of his home in Callao, the writing case, the little compartment in red velvet reserved for his pen. He went through the rooms, stopped to rest in his daughter's bedroom. She was sitting by the window that looked over the bay. He thought of Montse, who liked to use that pen, because the ink flowed so nicely, and then of his wife, and his daughter again. She had nibbled on it with her baby teeth, leaving marks in the gold. He thought of all this, for a brief moment. It was his last thought. The dust was soaking up his blood.

The son screamed. The penis fell out of his mouth. He still had the taste of his father's blood and semen on his tongue. He must be killed too, the Inca demanded, not even remotely joking now. But suddenly there were shots. Workers fell. The police had arrived. The cook had alerted them after dropping his silver platter. The crowd was decimated, men and women hit indiscriminately. It didn't take long for someone to finger the gang leader, the Inca. And it didn't take much longer to execute him as he stood alone near the shed that was burning out. They left his body to sear on the ground, between the blackened planks. The vultures came. His wife was raped behind the house by a policeman. A small assembly of the forces of order stood around. She was very pretty.

❧

The news reached the Spanish fleet anchored in the Mexican port of Manzanillo. Simón was resting his elbows on the ship's railing looking out over the bay. The indigo water soaked up the sun, which barely reverberated to tan the skin or blind the eyes.

It was one of the times in the day when Montse came to him. Although that was pretty much any time. In the free time after his reports and fabrications. Simón's mind always welcomed her as she was and as he made her.

1. As he made her: his memory had taken a few years off her lips, made her eyes stormier. Her voice remained a whisper, with no rise in tone, as if she were talking to him with her head on a pillow. She smelled like honey, a dose of sweetness that soothed him, and pepper, a dose of spice that excited him.
2. As she was: the bosom – a dose of spice – the hair, the spark.

Simón turned his thoughts to her daily. They were few enough of them, but each one lingered. He imagined their life together.

Sometimes even their children's lives. Sometimes he set his fantasies in Spain, sometimes America, less often Peru – so many settings, all of which turned into the bedroom, eventually.

Montse existed more fully for Simón in her absence. The anticipation of a reunion is often sweeter than the reunion itself, because you picture yourself saying everything that needs to be said, doing everything that needs to be done – after a painful wrench when the distance is created, the redeeming advantage is that you can't be rebuffed. You're no longer afraid to express yourself – how would you put it? – to allow everything you want to say to emerge from within – a flight of lyricism, a dissonant serenade – not squelching any desires or holding back any thoughts, with everything advancing the cause – enthusiasm (fake), poetry (plagiarized), singing (off-key) – with every answer from the object of your affection being yes (invented).

This is how Simón kept the image of her alive from one dream to the next. He had grown accustomed to this image the way you grow accustomed to your wife, seeing her without passion, your heart bathed in peace, your head filled with tenderness, comfort and shared memories. Sometimes he caught himself worrying that he might see her again, for fear that his beautiful fabrication would disintegrate in front of his eyes. Because part of his soul remembered the turbulence in her eyes, the fire in her hair – the danger. It remembered the vortex that Montse inhabited, which his mind had calmed in reconstructing her. His feelings were safe from the flesh-and-blood woman.

All was calm on the ships.

Half-asleep men handled the rigging; others created the illusion of being alert by making intermittent rounds, zigzagging from a starting point to nothing at all, just because. Pinzón left them to it. He was working in his cabin with his captains, shouting, knitting his eyebrows, pointing to a chart decorated with arrows and red circles that were spreading.

At last he said that the situation was serious – not overly serious, but serious enough. He had received some information, initially hearsay, but which he was able to correlate with a piece of gossip. Then there was plenty of corroboration, from drunks, of course, but lots of drunks. Rumour plus rumour equals fact.

There had been shore leave the night before, and the men had felt they should go into town. Simón had gone drinking with his shipmates. They had had a lot to drink; him not so much. This is how it went: he had taken care of a drunken sailor, then the same sailor again, then a friend of the sailor who was the ship's boy. Gradually, he had become the official saviour of anyone drowning in the bottle. A lifebuoy, the one on whom you threw yourself as the waters of your stupidity were rising. In the absence of a nurse, it fell to him. He eventually started to take the role seriously. Because it was nice to have responsibilities that gave your life meaning, a sense of nobility. So you drink less, you rise to the role, and you forget to have fun.

And in this sort of scenario, the party can start to drag on.

To amuse himself, Simón talked to the locals – bar owners and purveyors of services. Everyone was talking about the Spanish blood spilled in Peru. They mentioned one death, sometimes two. Always Spaniards. We thought it might interest you, you know, compatriots. Five pesos, or six – it was a small price to pay for information from the brother of the Mexican ambassador to Chile, all of it true, I swear.

When he returned, Simón repeated all of this to Admiral Pinzón, who made inquiries with officials and the locals. Nothing could be confirmed but the rumours. Certain details had even been added to the story: an organ severed, Inca vengeance, lascivious Peruvian police.

At around two o'clock in the afternoon, Pinzón had had enough. He sent the captains back to their ships and went out on deck.

He called for his men.

The captains did the same.

And on each boat simultaneously, they announced that they would be turning around, would be turning around, be turning around. In truth, they weren't really in synch. Pinzón had started late, at once uncertain and passionate about his decision, and wanting to find a bit of shade from the sun. He was also angry about the idea of backtracking. They had already seen the Central American coast and, frankly, it was nothing to write home about.

But it was such an insult, for Spain, for Spain!

The men listened as much to the speech being made on the other ships as to Pinzón's. It was well written, down to the last comma, and it was patriotic. It worked well without the silliness of the repetition. It was as if a parrot were hiding under a pile of canvas and rehearsing, half-smothered.

They finally understood the crux of the message: Peru had offered them the affront they had been waiting for. The scientific expedition was over, except perhaps when it came to medicine and ballistics. They would not be seeing San Francisco.

On deck, Simón thought of the letter he had not yet been able to start. He had spent so many hours rolling the pen between his fingers without putting it to paper, or doing so unconvincingly: prone, thrown, hurtled, dropped, but with the tip, no. He wouldn't need to write it now. Maybe deep down he had always known that they would be seeing Peru again. Maybe he had been anticipating this news even more than all of Spain had.

What a disgrace for our country! What an insult! the parrots cried. And Simón barely managed to arrange his face into the appropriate anger.

❧

It didn't take as long for the news to anger Callao. The brother recounted the horror upon his return. He was looking for someone to seek redress from, someone to blame, someone to be brought to justice, consequent hangings. Others calmed him down, explaining that it was an unfortunate incident, that the instigator had been punished by the police, his wife had too, several times. Was she rotting in jail? She would rot all right, make no mistake about it, after giving birth and the adoption, naturally, the worst jail with the worst guards. Guards so sinister you couldn't tell them from the criminals.

Montse was reading when her brother burst into her room. He was muddy (murdering a carpet) and bloody (here lies the bedding). He tracked dirt over fabric that would never recover. He explained almost the whole story, then asked her to talk about her books, right away, about her projects. It would take his mind off things.

Montse offered up theories about trauma, childhood, dreams and insomnia. They talked about possible worlds, those in our heads and the one before our eyes. The brother talked again about what he had seen: the spitting, the violence, the blood-soaked crepes. He didn't dare mention his father's penis.

Do you really think that world was in my head, Montse?

No, she said. Our heads create more beautiful worlds than that.

He told her that he hoped with all his heart that she was right. And that he was afraid to say what he saw in his head now. When I close my eyes, I see that world again, do you understand? And it seemed to him he would no longer be able to look at the world before his eyes much at all, even when it was calm, even when it was beautiful. He would have liked to ram a pretty panorama into his head, but it wouldn't fit; it resisted. He was confused. The ugliness in his head was there all the time, and it was knocking. It wanted to come out.

Then he told her that it was as if it were going to escape and take over his life, and that the outside world would become the inside world. Like that, everywhere, like that.

And Montse, who was afraid, pretended to listen to him. She took refuge in her thoughts. Finally, she asked him if he remembered the Murcia bell tower.

That evening, Montse put on a long black dress that covered her up to her neck and flattened her bosom. For the first time she wore a mantilla, which barely sparked when it came into contact with her hair. She didn't cry, but her eyes were clouded over. It was as though the sparkle, the stars, the mosquitoes' daredevil acrobatics had disappeared.

6

On November 13, 1863, the fleet saw Callao again. Slow progress on the sea gave them a chance to explain the situation to Madrid and let all of Europe know about the new manoeuvres. And to send Simón's latest reports, which told of a particularly strong cheese and much weaker wordplay. The ship's men even had enough time to grow weary of their rage and nearly forget about it. Headwinds had these sorts of discouraging effects.

But finally they arrived.

The sailors noticed the calm in Callao. The brazenness of unpunished laziness. Its docks dipping in the water like toes in the Pacific. And the flag flying at the top of the hill – not the Spanish flag.

They felt provoked once again. They found the rage they had misplaced. And Pinzón didn't make them feel any more forgiving by pointing out that the women of the town hadn't even come down to the port. No hankies, no goodbyes last time. It was no Chile, as they say.

There was no welcome party this time either. Pinzón hurried to disembark from the *Resolución*, even helping to put the gangway in place. He headed toward city hall, his head bent, eyebrows so knit that they touched and formed a bouquet of soot in the middle of his forehead. Dark ideas proliferated at that very spot. Simón could barely keep up with him, and the captains, who had once been young, abandoned the race. They would catch up; they would read about it in the report.

Along the way, they encountered a welcome party that was assembling. Under the mayor's direction, they were trying to pin rosettes on hats and untangle banners. Once they spotted Pinzón, a trumpet struck up the *Marcha Real*. It was quickly silenced by his look, and a bit by the jostling as they cut a path through the Peruvians. Admiral, said the mayor, to what do we owe the honour? What a nice … you seem a bit …

I need to see Mr. Pezet, Pinzón said.

He continued on his way, pursued by Simón, then the mayor, then a banner, then the trumpet player.

Pinzón finally went into city hall, chose the roomiest armchair in the entrance hall and plopped himself down in it. Simón stood near the rhododendron. Between sentences, he wondered if Montse ever came here, calculating his chances of running into her. Without knowing it, he increased them tenfold.

Well, Pinzón said, where is Pezet?

He's on tour, the mayor explained, on a presidential tour. He greets people, goes to the theatre.

Still the same play? Pinzón asked.

The question made things awkward. Yes, well, yes; he had very much enjoyed the one from the other night. Do you recall? Pinzón said that he did; it was hard to forget such a turkey, such a royal turkey. Not a bird native to Spain.

Out of the corner of his eye Pinzón looked at Simón, who was taking notes.

He continued, pushing, demanding that Pezet put an end to his tour. The real world needed him. In any case, it needed him a lot more than did Juanita, who seemed perfectly happy with Alessandro. For once the president's fantasies could come second to country.

Pinzón immediately asked Simón to strike out the word *country*. *The land* would be better, or *the people*, perhaps *his duties*. They would see. Fine, the mayor allowed. We'll alert President Pezet.

Very good.

But you should know that he is in Tarapoto, the City of Palms. And?

The mayor explained that a dispatch would take time, as would reading it, the trip, his arrival … time.

We'll wait here, Pinzón answered, his eyebrows doing the pile-of-coal thing again.

The mayor acquiesced but suggested it might not be necessary to sleep here, on the sofas. It would be better to return to the ships. No matter, no matter, Pinzón repeated.

Then he asked if the palm trees in Tarapoto were really that pretty. They must be since the city was nicknamed for them. That's something. What exactly is it about them? The mayor said that they were truly magnificent, tall and strong. The wind rustled their leaves, mimicking the sound of the sea, a rough sea, a storm. Oh, said Pinzón. Yes, said the mayor, a real squall. When you close your eyes, there are more storms in Tarapoto than in any port city in the Americas. Oh, Pinzón said again, you haven't seen Salamanca. I was referring to the Americas, the mayor said, the Americas. You're talking about Europe. But you haven't seen Salamanca, Pinzón said.

They were quiet. They waited.

The captains, who had lost their way, joined the threesome. They didn't know how they got lost, but they did know how they got found. A trumpet player had guided them, a good Samaritan. He played the *Marcha Real* rather well. They had listened to be polite.

Hours passed; the mayor excused himself at the end of one of them.

Gentlemen, my family.

The sun was setting when they decided to head back to the ships. They were hungry and tired. Their eyes, which periodically counted the ceiling tiles, spent longer and longer hidden behind eyelids; pins and needles invaded their hands, which tapped sword hilts to keep them at bay. They grew pensive. The smile of a woman left behind came to them, or fantasies of the woman they had never met, the One, who would surely come along, otherwise there was the fear of dying alone. It must have been the place that conjured such mythical creatures. So empty and calm it summoned wild thoughts. The silence, combined with the effects of the journey, the things they had seen, too much space. It mustn't be easy living in the Americas all the time, and it being the only place you could roam. Did they resign themselves to never seeing it all? Did they ever get used to their own insignificance, to the incredible vastness that reduces men to nothing?

No.

Let's go, Pinzón said. He was feeling suffocated; this would take some time. Pezet wanted to say goodbye to his palm trees and his turkey first.

On the way back, the admiral asked Simón not to mention this retreat. You should say that we waited, not sleeping; that's more real-istic, more determined, more Spanish. And our resolve is worthy of the fabrication. There is no point in exhausting ourselves right away. We will exhaust ourselves when fatigue is no longer an option.

ᘓ

Pezet never came. His tour was bringing him glory, and Juanita was weakening. He also loved the palm trees of Tarapoto. So he sent an envoy, Manuel Ignacio de Vivanco, the general. The stylish one.

The meeting took place a few days after the fleet's arrival, in the office of the mayor, who, for the cause, had graciously agreed to slip out. Pinzón asked the captains to wait in the entrance hall. He preferred the nobility of the duel, a steely face-to-face confrontation; it was a question of honour. So they went back to the ceiling tiles they had started counting the other day, counting the floor tiles when those ran out, and contemplating their lives.

But not you, Pinzón said.

Not me? Simón asked.

Well, yes, you.

The admiral wanted him in the meeting; Simón would dispassionately record what each one said and would give each a copy of the interview. A witness, it was customary; well, customary for a certain era, and this subcontinent was stuck in another century, so one had to adapt.

Vivanco smoothed his moustache, rolled one of its points between his fingers – pause – understood nothing, but didn't let it show, and then, saying to himself, These damn Spaniards, accepted.

You will take notes, Pinzón said.

I will take notes, Simón said.

Everything in the office was either beige or brown: a brown globe, a beige love seat, brown books, and at one end of the room, there was a large window striped with brown Venetian blinds, which filtered the beige light. The mayor's family portrait filled an entire section of the wall. The wife looked chubby, the child too, as did everything else in the portrait: the ottoman, the cushion, the canary. They blended in with the blandness of the mayor's chair, made of brown padded leather, a plumpish piece of furniture as wide as it was high, which unfortunately had survived the closing of a club, much to the chagrin of the aesthetes, and had run aground here after an auction. Vivanco sat in it, wondering whether he should lie down in it – pause – finally seeking comfort in an in-between position sometimes seen among opium addicts – further pause – and ending up sitting stiffly at right angles at the edge of the chair, so as not to surrender the propriety of discomfort, which was inevitable at any rate.

This made him look tall and skinny, as if deformed by the portrait or the armchair, a distorting effect that made Simón worry that he appeared just as absurd. Vivanco invited Pinzón to sit across from him. Pinzón declined, fearing he too would be the victim of visual distortion, concerned that the ottoman would narrow his jawbone and foil the effect of his sideburns, but above all he was angry enough to grant no further civilities. The past few days, spent ruminating and brooding, had made him impatient, and he wanted them to get to the point.

He nonetheless accepted the cigar that was offered to him, a Cuban.

Well, said Pinzón, we would like an apology and restitution.

He was standing near the portrait; it made him look taller. He was smoking, which made him look taller still, as if his head were sticking out of a cloud. Like a giant.

No apology is required, Vivanco replied. This is a domestic matter. Peru will deal with Peru.

Pinzón was fumigating the mayor's family and the canary.

We're talking about Spanish citizens, he said.

They had been living here for over twenty years, Vivanco reminded him.

Blood is blood, Pinzón said. Spain doesn't forget her sons and daughters.

She forgets other things, Vivanco said. Her defeats, for instance.

But not what she is owed, Pinzon said. Money and interests were stolen from her.

And he pulled a few dates from the drawers of History. Misunderstandings forty-two years old. He stressed that it was nothing personal; he smoked. Vivanco explained that Peru would not give in to blackmail any more than she would to asphyxia. It was nothing personal, he stressed further. Then there was a silence that the smoke seemed to be sketching in the air: nervous scrolls, uncertain arabesques that surrounded Pinzón and Vivanco, containing nothing recognizable, no answer or clue, no moustache or eyebrows, no dragon or cauldron that could have been the source of these thick clouds ...

I will report this to Madrid, Pinzón finally said.

And I will report this to Lima, Vivanco said.

Yes, Pinzón said, losing his temper, report this to Lima, go ahead. Or rather to Tarapoto; you will have a better chance of being heard. If the palm trees will pipe down, of course.

And he pointed out that Juanita did not have to be briefed about all this.

That was it.

Vivanco was indignant, got up from the armchair, and then turned his back on Pinzón. He peered through the smoke and the jealousy, absorbed. He would have liked to see a carnival going on outside, to show the Spaniards that life here was doing very well without them. Death too. But the square was empty. Aside from two dogs and a wounded bird that they were tearing limb from limb: a wing was folding and unfolding like a fan as it was shaken, a foot left on the ground would soon become a good-luck charm. Head, beak, eye were of no particular use now – the quartering went on, blood staining feathers and muzzles. The dogs were wearing collars. They must belong to someone. They should be better trained.

Stratus clouds, Vivanco finally said. You should take an umbrella when you go. A gift. It will be big enough for the both of you.

Simón still wanted to make a copy of the talks to give to Manuel Ignacio de Vivanco.

That won't be necessary, Pinzón said.

That's fine, Vivanco acquiesced. We won't forget any of this.

Finally something they could agree on. It could have been the cornerstone for a compromise, but no. Instead they left, slamming the door behind them. In the lobby, they collected the captains, who were starting to worry about their fate and the tiles, and they headed back to the ships, taking neither French leave nor English leave but Spanish leave, which is a great deal noisier. Pinzón was angry that he hadn't taken an umbrella, because the rain was cold, and that he had left Spain, because Peru was ridiculous.

Salazar

1864

7

They alerted Madrid again.

Madrid took the news hard. Isabelle neglected her little dog, quintupled her meringue intake, blamed her deputy ministers between mouthfuls. They thought Pinzón, the poor beggar, in spite of his prestigious lineage, was failing to command respect. They concluded just as logically that, since Peru wasn't yielding, they would have to ask for more. For example, the repayment of debts from the war of independence, a war they suddenly remembered.

But poor Pinzón, Pinzón whose bloodline wasn't sufficient to make himself heard. Columbus had managed to make the natives understand immediately that he was the best person to safeguard their interests. It just went to show that, sometimes, to communicate with those people, you have to stop talking. You have to do something else. And Pinzón seemed to be sorely lacking in something else. The poor beggar.

So they sent Eusebio de Salazar y Mazarredo to explain all this to the Peruvians. It was an impressive name, further enhanced by the title of royal commissioner. He was not an ambassador, it should be noted, but a commissioner; and not a commissioner of nothing at all, but a royal one, therefore not of a country but of a colony.

The war of independence was already fading from memory.

⁂

Eusebio de Salazar y Mazarredo arrived in Peru in March 1864 aboard a ship sent to reinforce Pinzón's fleet. The crossing was made in record time — oh, the madness of modernity — and the news of escalating tensions made the rounds of the world's papers: Paris, London, Moscow, Madrid.

Salazar boarded the *Resolución*.

He was very much of his time: the beard, the pomade, the uniform dripping with decorations and festoons forming spirals on his shoulders. He looked like a theatre. He looked as though his chest and armpits were going to open up on to a performance.

As the ranking officer on deck, who had come that day to get the ship's news at the request of the captain of the *Triunfo*, Simón introduced himself and explained Pinzón's absence. He was fuming in his cabin, planning, fuming some more, finally throwing a sextant out the porthole, then tracing an umpteenth red circle on his yellow chart. Very well, Salazar said, let's go join him; let's see what's going on.

The play was starting.

Salazar emerged from the chart room the next day. His cheeks were red, and the whites of his eyes were yellow. He had coloured hard, even broken a few navigation tools. He asked Simón to accompany him; the admiral had spoken highly of his calligraphy, and a meeting was planned with Peruvian officials. They wanted to settle the crisis, but it seemed likely it would be aggravated instead, and hopes were turning to dust. Pinzón stayed with his charts to scribble on them some more.

They were received in the mayor's office in Callao by Juan Ribeyro. He was the minister of foreign affairs.

They asked for Pezet. Pezet was off somewhere chasing his dreams They demanded to see Vivanco. Vivanco had had enough of the Spaniards: he was in Lima seeing to his dogs, recent acquisitions he was trying to train.

The meeting was unproductive. Simón was there in body but not in spirit. He jotted down a few snatches of a conversation that never really got off the ground. Greetings, absence, silence. Carpets of silence that unfurled longer and longer. Simón barely noticed them. He was thinking of himself – well, of what was alive inside him, a long way from the carpets, his head too full of sounds and the occasional image. Yes, that one.

They commented on the chubby portrait. Nice roundness, nice rendering. Then the commissioner officially introduced himself. Ribeyro replied that he would have liked to receive an *ambassador* within these walls. That Peru was getting a bit offended by this selective memory.

What was that supposed to mean?

That they remembered independence when it came to debts, but not when it came to protocol. That they were giving themselves phony titles, if you really must know.

Ah, retorted Salazar, look who's talking. A minister of foreign affairs, when everyone here is a son of Spain. The only thing that seemed foreign was the attitude of Mr. Pezet, who preferred the theatre to diplomacy.

They drank some Tokay to lighten the mood. It became so light that they talked only about the portrait, a little about the tempestuous palm trees in Tarapoto, from time to time about the president of Chile, deemed eccentric. Everything had already been said, but no one dared admit it. So a second Tokay, small talk, clearing of throats, waiting for half past the hour to make it seem as though the meeting had had a point. At half past, it was hard to cut things short without admitting to themselves that they had failed, so they drank more to summon the courage to make the failure official and leave.

After the fourth drink, their heads started spinning, and they felt that control of the future had slipped from their grasp. They understood that war could no longer be avoided. What they understood less was why. Once the insults were exchanged, the grievances itemized, the subject changed, what was left other than reconciliation? But war is a slippery slope, they thought; once declared, there was no going back without the great effort of climbing back up the hill. So let's let things run their course, not so much because our differences are insurmountable but because, we might as well admit it, we are all lazy in our own ways — imagine explaining it to the newspapers. And wasn't it almost heartening to pick up a long-dormant conflict right where we left off? It was like an old couple giving in, a couple who no longer work to stay together, who are essentially bored by peace, and who for lack of anything better to do fan the flames.

But this time to the bitter end, they promised, until someone surrenders. Deluding themselves about the well-being and the sense of levity that would follow, fantasizing about the post-apocalyptic peace that castle ruins offered a taste of.

For the time being, all was calm. They said nothing. They needed inspiration before the shouting and the blame. They were just waiting for someone to stand up and get things rolling. Or a noise that would snap them out of their bitter reverie, in which they were already preparing new accusations.

Simón didn't know it right then, but History had begun its march in front of his eyes, a bit idiotic and mad, germinating with things that drunk men do or don't do. But how was he to know? History had been too silent, like a woman who suddenly ups and leaves, taking the future with her. Shouldn't the warning have been louder? Clearer, to be sure, than long evenings spent inside their heads, without smiling at one another? The men would blame each other the rest of their lives. They didn't see the clues. Perhaps they had been thinking about themselves a little too much, shut away in their slight uncertainty. They would have to forgive themselves. Because History has been fooling men since the dawn of time. It is built on trivial things that come and go, and that no one notices, like the tide.

The men in turn began their march. Their agitation was dulled by the alcohol. Their reflexes too. Hands sought support on the armchair, then on the doorframe. Then on the shoulder of a passing civil servant. Ribeyro and Salazar crossed the lobby this way, seeing each other to the door of city hall. Behind them, Simón tried to follow their complicated advance, moving slowly toward a pedestal table, the exit, a rhododendron, the exit.

※

Within the larger frame of History, Simón was living his own little story.

He wanted to see Montse again.

He wrote her notes. Their tenderness was veiled in amusing tidbits scattered through the sentences, like small defensive walls that would protect him from a response that was too passionate, prevent him from exposing himself to what he metaphorically called 'a desert wind' – what he meant was clearly the barren feeling of a refusal. So an anecdote protected the 'see you again,' a witticism minimized the significance of the 'evening under the umbrella.'

He rewrote most of the notes.

Then he tried to have them delivered to her. Sometimes by a sailor, which didn't work at all. A florist wandering the docks, pfft. A small boy whose confiscated hoop served as a means of barter: nada.

Montse had not responded.

The weeks of forced confinement in port grew longer; Simón's worry increased proportionately. What could she possibly have against him? Why the silence? Had he invented what happened that night, the feelings it had given rise to? He thought about asking for shore leave to go to her house. Would it be unseemly?

His questions could be summed up in a simple line that he had scribbled at the bottom of a report one night when he couldn't sleep:

Did I fall in love with a dream?

One Sunday, at the end of the afternoon, there were developments. It was the evening before the fateful meeting where Simón had recorded nothing. Salazar had just come aboard the ship. He was talking to Pinzón. Tomorrow they would meet Ribeyro with no great hope of reconciliation. So let's seethe, my dear Pinzón, let's scheme.

Simón walked along the docks, on the verge of giving up, when he saw a woman dressed in black approaching. It was the Ortuño maid. She was walking in little hops, talking in little chirps. She greeted the florist, an acquaintance, and the young boy, a nephew, whose reclaimed hoop had fallen in the water.

She stopped in front of Simón, slipped him an envelope hidden in the palm of her hand. It was from Mademoiselle. Then she hopped back to the town, disappeared, chirping all the way. You should have steered your hoop better. You have to be careful with what you have in life. Otherwise you end up with nothing to entertain you as you head into old age. Nothing but thoughts and memories. Which are dangerous.

Simón looked at the sealed letter for a moment – burgundy wax, initials formed with dizzying spirals – and then carefully opened it. His heart was beating too loudly for him to read. He forced himself to stay calm, remembered his alphabet. He finally recognized an A, and then the letters that followed.

Montse explained that her brother was not well. She had to take care of him. They had left a month before for Lambayeque to see, to collect themselves, perhaps to understand. The shed had been rebuilt.

Simón couldn't understand what she meant. His mind was dulled by desire.

Finally, Montse added that they had returned the night before.

> Could we see each other for a moment? Come to my house in an hour. We'll go for a walk.
>
> M
>
> P.S. I would have preferred letters. I waited for your letters. I received only notes.

Simón immediately raised his defences, just in case.

I knew I would see you again.

Simón rang the bell. The maid answered. He spotted Montse behind her, at the end of the corridor. She didn't know what she wanted, hesitating between the peace of her books and the whirlwind of life.

The maid formally announced Lieutenant Claro. This may have given Mademoiselle a little push.

It was little indeed. Montse approached slowly. It was all she could do to smile. She tried to muster a convincing welcome to offer this man who was so nice, after all, who deserved it. He had come all this way.

Simón understood. Like the maid, Montse was dressed in black. She was wearing a mantilla like a spider web on her hair, which, tied back, no longer sheltered her face. Her fragility showed clearly on it: eggshell chin, cheeks red from the day that was fading. Other delicateness he recognized: the dewy eyes, the wafer-like nose – the naked bird.

The woman from the gala was barely recognizable. It was like identifying one's mother in old photographs from the details. It was her eye, her nostril, her freckle.

It's you.

They wandered the streets.

Montse said that indeed her father had been killed. She was in mourning. The house had never been so full of the sounds of clocks ticking and feet stepping. They were treading lightly around each other, afraid of disturbing each other's grief.

Simón repeated his condolences and support. It became a sort of prayer.

At times, no longer able to stand hearing himself, he stopped talking, looked Montse in the eye, held her gaze for a few seconds.

He repeated the same sadness in the silence, but it seemed easier to hear. Then Montse smiled more genuinely. A half smile, that is.

And, without knowing what from his past made him empathize, she knew that he understood. It soothed her a little that her pain – yes, her disappointment and her fatigue, too – were shared. Sorrow brings people closer than joy, and in being shared, one can lead to the other.

They even managed to laugh once or twice. Oh, about nothing, a silly detail glimpsed when detouring down an alley or the shape of a cloud. Really, it looked like a piece of fruit, a shell, a witch. Or John Rodgers, when you look at it the other way around.

Once the distraction had passed, Montse continued describing the state of her soul and the house. She feared for her brother, who was behaving oddly at night and in the things he said. It was if he were travelling inside himself, turning away from his mind to drift until he was lost. Then he would yell, *Where am I, where are you, bring me back.* He wandered farther and farther, and his yelling grew fainter, a mere breath sometimes, mad muttering.

He was disguised too, always disguised. Oh, not in costumes, but his face, his eyes, his words, all three of them furtive.

He wanted to be someone else, someone who is gone and cannot be disturbed.

Montse thought he could be suffering from a psychological trauma. She consulted her books but couldn't diagnose anything specific. She would have to study it. Maybe she could write about it. Discover something new.

Chance brought them to the edge of the town. Now they were walking along the coast, following a narrow mule path. Montse no longer spoke of her pain. She was silent or, without expecting a response, she would comment on nature, a tree, the wind, the emptiness. Her words got lost in it all; they were too small.

Simón walked behind her. He matched her slow step, hardly complaining at all. He could see the waves swell and break; he could watch the gulls dropping sea urchins onto the rocks; he could run his eyes up and down Montse's neck, which, laid bare by the sudden gusts of wind that foiled the forbidding nature of the muslin, turned out to be delicate, smooth, pure. A small stretch of snow extinguished by the coal black of the dress. To run his eyes up and down again and imagine his hand on that forbidden skin, squeezing, pressing a little, feeling her flesh. His palm touching the bumps of the vertebrae, his fingertips absorbing the pulse of the jugular.

You didn't write me long letters, Montse finally said. Nice ones.

The wind had died down enough to let her talk.

I knew I would see you again, Simón answered.

Finally they climbed the hills. Grey clouds dusted the sky, which was so low that it brushed their heads.

Simón tried to talk about the war that was looming, about the shadow that the Spanish masts cast over the town. A fist of hatred was slowly squeezing the day-to-day lives of the citizens of Callao, the salons, the carambolas, Sundays.

What do you think about it? Not much. Will the town be crushed? It's hard to say.

Don't be here if it happens.

All right, Montse answered.

But their thoughts took them elsewhere. Another fist was squeezing them. It was their own little drama, so close that it blinded them.

Engulfed by this sea of worry, they preferred to swim in the pool of their own desire. They believed they were in danger of drowning in it, maybe wanted to, to avoid the tragedy that Spain was going to visit upon Peru. One storm protected them from the other.

So they spoke of Pinzón to get back to Diego, mentioned Madrid to talk again about theatre, or about the umbrella and the lights of the port.

Do you remember?

They headed toward a coastal battery, the only building in sight. They soon reached a steep path, and Simón had to help Montse, to hold her hand as she jumped over a wooden barrier. He remembered the first evening, when she had surprised him in the doorway of her house to lead him inside, further into an adventure that he had believed over. The alabaster of the dress may be gone, he thought, and perhaps the alabaster of her soul too, but the alabaster of her hands certainly was not, nor was their softness. Some bodies can survive the extinction of the soul. And some souls can survive the disintegration of the body. One or the other was inevitable, Simón thought, just as Juvenal dreamed. Which should we hope to lose first?

They approached the battery. Fog rose up from the sea. The fortifications were being watched less than diligently by two men smoking outside. They were walking and disappearing behind patches of fog that skimmed the hilltops like great nets and then moved on, having caught nothing.

Simón and Montse sometimes passed through these diaphanous walls. They lost sight of each other in them and then reappeared to one another, thrilled to find themselves together again, to be reunited, to know that they were still indeed there, despite the fact that it would have been impossible to disappear. It was ridiculous, really, just as it was ridiculous to doubt for a moment. But their hearts were glad.

They walked along the beige cement wall surrounding the fortification. They had run out of small talk. So they stopped talking, perhaps out of fear of dissipating a dream that was rolling in with the fog.

Now they were side by side, and the rocks and the uneven ground caused them to bump into each other every so often. They didn't even try to walk straight. They gently collided, hips, shoulders. Heat found heat, mingled before separating, leaving a subtle glow on their skin, and a not-so-subtle blaze in their minds.

Montse finally leaned back against the beige wall. It was uncomfortable because it was rough. She slid her hands under her bottom. Her black dress looked like a new opening in the low, pale wall, a dark door to the other side that had suddenly appeared.

I imagined a few of your letters.

And what did they say?

They talked about your travels.

A cloud shrouded Montse. When she reappeared, they were looking each other in the eye, each with the impression that this lovers' game was only perpetuating the pain and indecision. Simón saw that Montse's eyes were growing dull, the sparkle was gone. And Montse noticed in Simón the ever-so-slight doleful moistening of the eye, a welling up of the expectation that she no longer had the strength to fill. It is easy to understand why people close their eyes to pluck up their courage – which they did at the same time.

Uneasiness enveloped them more than the fog and the dream. Simón wanted to kiss Montse. It was a noble desire: to catch hope before it fell, to break through the mask of routine, to seize the truth before propriety returned, to never go back to life. But all the black that Montse had on, on her body, in her face, her eyes, was an obstacle to his desire. Simón was afraid of falling into it, like the other night in the harbour water.

And then there were the clouds that were coming lower, dusting their shoulders; there was the wind that tore his cocked hat from the head and the will from his mind. There was the wall she was leaning against, melted, transformed, surrounding her like a nun watching. The world was conspiring against their kiss.

There was to be no further movement, either in body or mind. They would have to try in words.

Write me, Montse said, write me.

So you're giving me another chance.

Well, the second and last one.

He thanked her. And it was only natural that they go back down, because there was nothing more to do up there and the fog was growing thicker, keeping them shrouded longer and longer.

They were exhausted.

Maybe something was rolling in with the fog. It was just something invisible: enthusiasm or hope or desire.

They took the same detours that they had taken the first night, replayed the silences. Once they were in front of her door, Montse squeezed Simón's arm gently. He hoped she would take him inside. If only hope were enough.

The maid was waiting for them. She opened the door, and Montse disappeared into the hallway. The maid closed the door slowly. She looked at Simón, who didn't meet her eye. Instead he saw Montse disappear into the darkness of the hall as if her dress, becoming unstitched with each step, were returning to the fabric of the night. A black, starless night, but so beautiful in spite of it all. A beautiful darkness, oh my.

Simón took the road back to the *Triunfo*. He wondered why all those years of study, travel and chess had not helped him read his own heart. What did it want? What should he do? Would this lesson one day end?

He wanted to see her again. And he made every deal possible with God. He promised to give his future fortune to beggars, to go to church every Sunday and to be strict with himself at Lent. He offered a solemn vow to protect her. He swore on his soul.

He had done this only four times before.

Then he went back to his big dreams of love. Ideals long dead were resurrected, he was an adolescent again. To see her again that way, to want to see her yet again, ah, Simón knew he would have a hard time sleeping.

꒰

They weighed anchor two days later, after the meeting with the Tokay, at dawn and without warning. It surprised Peru as much as it did Simón. History was intermingling with his own smaller story.

See, Pinzón has a plan, Salazar explained. It was hard to decipher on the chart, after so much rage and so many red circles. But the drawing was pretty.

8

They saw three fingers pointing, the fingers of a large cadaver that had been buried at sea and partially exhumed by the currents. It was the Chincha Islands. It was hard to fully comprehend that after so much archery and acrobatics with the charts, the Spanish intervention could boil down to a pile of loose stones.

Pinzón had been evasive when he addressed the crews.

1. After many doodles and sleepless nights, the officers had reached a consensus.
2. The islands were essential to Peru's economy; so they'd seize them.
3. Spain would thus force those guilty of sedition to pay the compensation demanded; and of course there was the question of Honour.

If that didn't work, they would suggest trading the three rocks for a larger one: Gibraltar. We will remove this thorn from Spain's side, Pinzón enthused. Which would relieve a sixty-year-old malaise. Which would impose their way of thinking on the maps of the world and simplify matters for cartographers. The Portuguese aberration would follow.

Simón liked islands, in general. And these particular ones couldn't have been better timed. He gazed at them from the ship, his head filled with fantasies of escape, a simple life and love. Living there forever. Leaving the navy to just roam, forget Spain and think of nothing but Peru. With, deep down, the persistent idea of abducting Montse and building a hut out of palm fronds. Architectural prowess followed by passion in the sea.

The poor man had done too much reading, so now he was doing too much dreaming. *The Odyssey*, for example, had created an association for him between islands and carnal pleasure. Although he was having a hard time incorporating Atlantis into his imaginings – sorry, Plato – but no matter. The two of them wouldn't be forming a civilization. The point was to escape civilization.

Because Simón believed that their love would grow best surrounded by the sea and cut off from the world. Nothing could threaten it there, not lovers, not jealousy. His closest competitor would be simian.

And he indulged in a few more detailed scenarios. Montse sitting by his side on the beach, near their palm frond shelter. Moments of contemplation, a head on the shoulder, a hand on the forearm, and the purity of the ocean in front of them, the purity of the vegetation behind them. His body getting lost in hers.

He kept daydreaming of half-naked frolicking, of hunting and fishing – always successful – of long embraces to ward off the cold and similarly interminable sunsets. It was all the things he had read back at school, interspersed with all the things he had later read one-handed. Sunsets would backlight the tip of a nipple, purify the skin in its orange glow, make the shadow of a breast seem bigger. Tender embraces leading to rancid sweat.

And climaxing in the jungle and on the beach, where his seed would be dwarfed by all the surrounding life, would lose its indecency far from the austerity of closed doors. It was absorbed by the foam, extinguished by the spray, melting into it until it disappeared. And similarly, perversity gradually disappeared from his thoughts. And the pleasure his mind derived from the fantasy was dwindling in the same way. It was good timing. The islands were coming closer. War would be starting soon.

The island where they berthed looked nothing like his dream island. Rock had formed on it like layers of an onion. Agitation frozen by waving a magic wand, fountains turned to sediment in the night.

The troops came ashore, initially worried about whether the ground was solid, because it seemed to be boiling. Feet tested the rock. Let's go, move it along; come on, step lively! The officers set an example by hopping over the stones, then by wading through the mud along the side of the road. Every quagmire has a bottom, you see, there is always something firm hiding under something soft. Salacious laughter all around. Debauched characters, sleazy crew members, this is mucky business. More laughter. And you'll clean my boots. Silence.

They walked warily toward the village. It was dirty; the houses seemed to have been built out of soot and spit. The only shows of resistance were scowling faces and shutters slammed shut.

They searched the homes looking for weapons and pitchforks. They didn't find much, so they confiscated everything, down to the forks. Simón observed the operation; Pinzón directed it. You could see the beginnings of disappointment in his terse, fitful gestures. No blood, no accolades. The report of the operation would probably need a few changes.

Simón was one step ahead of him. In his notebook, he substituted guns for forks. Then he sketched the general atmosphere. A strange coating covered maybe not everything but plenty of things. The bricks were glazed with it, as were the wagons, and the hats, and the women's dresses. Even skin seemed permanently stained by it.

It was mysterious, threatening. No, not quite.

Overpowering, yes, that was it.

The troops were definitely in great danger – period. New paragraph.

They might encounter more resistance when they captured the governor. Pinzón had given the order, buoyed by the idea of drawing gunfire.

They lay siege to the villa, and they found Governor Ramón Valle Riestra at the table in front of a vol-au-vent. A few bites, gentlemen, if you don't mind. They allowed him the pleasure of finishing his peas, then he was led through the entrance hall, the square and the silence to the *Resolución*. His cabin was dark but comfortable. They took off his handcuffs to offer him a meal, but no thank you, he had already eaten.

The few scattered Peruvian troops that remained lay down their arms without protest. They had been discovered almost by chance, at a bend in a road, in the backyard of a municipal building, on the outskirts of the village, picking flowers. They had played a lot of cards.

Then came the traditional march and the raising of the Spanish flag. The march was a little embarrassing. They lacked the training for this sort of thing, the wherewithal as well. And, as everyone knows, sailors do not march well. Land is not their element. Stamping boots rather than snapping sails – we'll come back to it. Pinzón furrowed his brow and berated the captains, relieved that the only spectators were him and a handful of yokels peering from between the shutters.

The flag-raising was more successful. The wind did its bit, just enough. It blew without stealing the show. The flag curved like a proud, puffed-out chest, releasing its tension in the beautiful undulations of a belly dancer. Pinzón smiled. The captains did too. They struck up the *Marcha Real*. It rang through the silent air of the island – or almost silent because the sky was filled with birds. Strange birds that looked bizarre in flight and sang and cawed and kept circling without even noticing the Spaniards. Birds that just didn't care.

It was odd that this anthem broke their routine. Even more so since the trumpet player didn't play it very well. Nothing like the quality of the trumpet player in Callao who had so irritated them. But they appreciated it, and their chests did a fair imitation of the swell of the flag. Because they were the ones playing this time. Not an imposter.

They finished taking the island with a few hurrahs. Then the locals came out on their porches, went back about their business, which looked a good deal like aimless wandering. They stared at the occupiers without any real hatred; sadness, rather. For themselves, for the Spaniards blinded by heedlessness, for other reasons.

Pinzón was thrilled to see the people go back about their business as if nothing had happened. A master is a master. They caught on quickly at least, these Peruvians. No need for fires or terror campaigns. Maybe we'll distribute a few rifle butts in a bit. But nothing more.

Simón was still wondering.

What sort of work did they do? Where did the ones who were leaving the town in a group go, with their spades over their shoulders?

He went to Pinzón for an explanation. It would help him with his report. He couldn't see the point of occupying such a remote, hostile, dirty place.

You couldn't be more wrong, rejoiced Pinzón, contemplating his conquest.

These small islands, Lieutenant, represent 60 percent of the enemy's revenue. This is a serious blow. It's the arrow in Achilles' heel.

Although not in Achilles', in Peru's, he clarified, more the dart in the heel of a premature baby.

Simón was still confused.

Pinzón led him to the centre of the square where a fountain lay dormant. He ran his index finger along its stone border. It was covered with the same dust as everywhere else. His finger turned grey as though it had instantaneously rotted.

This dirt is used to make gunpowder, he said. It's used to make war.

Pinzón brought his finger close to Simón's face. Smell it. Smell it. You didn't say no to the admiral. Simón breathed in the index finger, which didn't smell like anything. So what was it?

Shit, Pinzón said.

And he headed back toward the ships, asking for his hanky.

Simón scanned the square, the village with its ashy tones. It was on the rocks, the buildings. On the men's hands.

He glimpsed the countryside in the distance. Residents and soldiers were starting up a game of orders and acrimony – some of the cries carried all the way to the fountain. Faster, harder.

The shit pervaded their hearts.

Pareja

1864–1865

9

Occupying three rocks wasn't enough. Life in Peru was pretty good: enough potatoes, sufficient vines, undisturbed peace. Most of the droppings collected on the islands were for export. Without conquering Lima, which could hold for a while, Spain was irritating the English, the Americans and Napoleon III, who had been abandoned in Mexico two years before. He had been insulted, backs had been turned on him on the pretext of a lack of funds, and, suddenly, we will forgive him for getting annoyed, Spain found the money to finance an expedition.

The Spanish Ambassador in Paris explained that this was for science and was surprised to see traces of doubt on the emperor's face.

Would he prefer we remain stuck in the Dark Ages?

We'll force their hand, Pinzón decided, the other hand. He left a few men behind and blockaded the main Peruvian ports. So few ships, so many places to land: sealing off the sea would be difficult. Ships simply sailed around the Spanish fleet. They slipped rather rudely past it in the night. So it was impossible to inspect anything other than a pleasure craft here, a fishing boat there, particularly since the *Triunfo* had had the poor judgement to sink. The Peruvians had nothing to do with the incident; it had been a drunken sailor indisposed by the north wind blowing down from the mountains. He thought it would be a good idea to light a fire in the rigging, and in the sails, to warm up even faster.

Panic spread faster than the flames. The crew evacuated the ship before the order was given. They had plenty of time to admire it as it went up in flames, telling themselves that maybe they could have, with buckets...

After drying off, Simón wrote his report. This time, no additions were requested. He even edited it down to make it more vague. The pyrotechnics became a mysterious accident that could have been caused by a seagull, a fish, the hand of God.

≫

But God was on Spain's side. So at the palace in Madrid, the latest report was considered most regrettable. Was that ridiculous Pinzón up to the job? Was Peru that well prepared?

Questions to which Ramón María Narváez y Campos, the new prime minister of Spain, answered no and no. In 1838, he had swept La Mancha clean of swarms of bandits. He didn't see the difference between them and the Peruvian armed forces: it was a question of organization, cleanliness, bad guys. Pinzón seemed to be cutting corners, botching the job; he didn't seem to know where to begin. To prove his worth, he was waiting for a battle that was no more likely to come to him than a genie. Why couldn't he understand that cockroaches don't stay in formation, that they don't confront the broom? You have to eliminate the shadows where they hide and annihilate them one by one by crushing them.

Isabelle II asked herself why not. It would be hard to do any worse than sinking your own ships. And Ramón María Narváez was neither hard on the ears nor the eyes. He had a moustache and big ears that his small sideburns didn't hide. He was also the first Duke of Valencia. He sold violence well; he sold it like mink. It was soft, it was warm and the animal hadn't suffered. On his death bed, four years later, the priest would ask him to forgive his enemies.

I don't have any, he would say. I had them all killed.

The diplomatic ranks were excited about this newcomer. Here is some of the fancy footwork that took place.

Those who had found Pinzón too tough now found him too soft. Narváez made even the most sullied hands appear lily white.

So they decided to replace the admiral – his distinguished bloodline would no longer suffice, and he wasn't spilling enough enemy blood.

Pinzón heard the news one evening as a Peruvian schooner was sticking out its tongue behind his blockade's back. He dismissed the officers from his quarters and shut himself in, waiting for his replacement. He would return to Spain aboard the first ship flying a neutral flag – or maybe he would go to the United States. Because John Rodgers had intrigued him. The civil war he had talked about did too.

His parting gesture was one of the eyebrow.

⁂

Juan Manuel Pareja and a few more ships arrived in Peru in December 1864. He was given command of the fleet aboard the *Villa de Madrid*, the new flagship, with no great pomp or enthusiasm. Sword, cracked note on the trumpet, raising of the flag – let's get on with it.

He was born in Lima but, after the Peruvian insurrections, everyone he knew went back to Spain. He had never followed fashion or sported a moustache. He hated what he called rebels and, more generally, anyone who wasn't a royalist.

His father had fought the Chilean revolutionaries in 1813. His death had had three acts:

1. There was the fire in Old Lope's barn where he had taken refuge;
2. There was the patience of revolutionary forces who surrounded the building;
3. There were the guns fired at the burnt body emerging from Old Lope's barn, sword drawn.

Juan had cried.
When asked about it later, he denied it.

Settling a family matter, Narváez believed, required the help of a member of that family. And in addition to the flaw of being Peruvian, Juan Manuel Pareja had the quality of being heartless. People already perceived him as having the same skin colour and ideas as the prime minister.

Also there was widespread surprise when, dismissing the theatre that had been Salazar – Madrid needs you, my good man – the admiral struck up new negotiations with Lima. It was thought to be for appearances. And it was, although substance was stirred up anyway, and Pareja increased his grievances threefold, increased his insults fivefold, logically increasing sevenfold his consumption of Cuban cigars. His demands grew exponentially, his aims even more extravagant than those of Pinzón and Salazar combined. They involved resources, promises, throw in some women, why not, and some Inca gold while we're at it.

President Pezet's envoy, Manuel Ignacio de Vivanco, explained clearly that they would concede no more today than they did yesterday. His opinion of the men was still as harsh, his moustache still as smooth – he had come back against his better judgement. He had been promised that the meeting would be short. He had had his ego stroked – pause –and ballast added to his purse. People said he knew how to talk to men.

I talk to them like dogs, he explained.

Surprisingly, they reached an agreement.

Pareja wanted to declare victory as soon as possible.

Vivanco was worried about the fate of Caramba and Calíope, his dogs, who were teething.

President Pezet was still thinking about Juanita.

The paperwork was signed aboard the *Villa de Madrid* one fine afternoon in January – there is such a thing. It was sunny and not too cold; the sea gave the men a chance to sleep in. It was calm to the point of being still, the energy hidden below the surface as if under a large white sheet. Sometimes the sea stirred with an eddy, or some backwash, as if shifting a knee or an arm.

It was 1865. The war had been going on for nine months already. The Spaniards had captured three islands and accidentally lost a ship. They had shot a man; their honour was intact.

❧

Lima took a dim view of the treaty. Too much had been conceded to the enemy: the islands, compensation payments and a great deal of pride. Speeches in the Chamber pitted people against one other. They all threw another log on the fire of general indignation. It went beyond the usual debate.

In the streets, things were less metaphorical. Stakes were erected to burn Pezet and Isabelle II in effigy, each in turn. The effigy of a widely hated local bigshot was sometimes added to the fire, depending on how whipped up the demonstrators were and on the inventory of available straw.

Congress refused to ratify the accord. The people had been heard. Or rather misheard. Because once news got out about the refusal, the people went back down into the streets for some rioting. They wanted the war to end, Spain to leave – who gives a damn about honour – and then if they could all the same give a good smack to the Cortéses, Pizarros and De Balboas over there. And all those Aguirres who come from the other world to sow evil in ours, amen.

The people were impossible to understand.

Nevertheless, Pezet's government would fall a few months later. Vivanco learned of it over the barking of his dogs.

Pezet learned of it during a performance that he interrupted abruptly before making his intentions known.

Juanita: No, Mr. Pezet, no, I won't come with you.

Pezet: But what if, Juanita, what if we fled this dismal reality to live out our dream.

Her name wasn't Juanita, but Anna María. She was, however, beautiful, and married to Alessandro, the actor. Pezet would have preferred fiction and reality be reversed.

He settled instead in Tarapoto, where he rarely spoke to women. First he would ask for their given name, then didn't believe them, pulled the ring finger of their left hand toward him, before they stalked off, incensed. Then he went back to listening to the palm trees.

10

Anyway, for a while Peru will play only a minor role in our story. It was the spark. But the true blaze of the war was obscuring other skies.

Pareja was informed that Pezet was deposed while his armada was already patrolling Chilean waters. The country that laid claim to these waters had gotten in a huff a few weeks earlier. Here's what happened.

The war was complicated. There had been threats, treaties, meetings, escalation. People were talking about Spanish arrogance and Peruvian indifference. But nothing was coming to a head – there was no conqueror, not even any battles really. It was a war that gave no one any peace, that spilled over a little into neighbouring countries like a dog barking in the next yard. Well, said Bolivia, Ecuador and Chile, what should we do?

Especially since Chile quite liked its president and had noticed how Spain had undermined Pezet's credibility in his own country so that his government had faltered. Hadn't the Spaniards questioned the suitability of our own president, Pérez, at a party? They remembered all too well a joke about his love of the ballet.

There was further discussion among the prominent families of Santiago, and then two or three scathing attacks published in the newspapers. It was becoming clear that Spain had come to restore its empire.

With so few ships?

With so little violence?

But with such arrogance – it was plain to see.

Pérez still believed in moderation. On the other hand, he was irritated at being ridiculed for his love of the ballet. So they wanted to help Peru a little and punish Spain just as little. It was only right.

Having a Castilian merchant navy ship in Chilean waters was the perfect opportunity to put this new policy into action. When those aboard the Spanish vessel asked for a little coal for their boilers, they were refused. Coal was a resource that could not be sold to a warfaring nation. Yes, things had taken an unfortunate turn, but President Pérez was determined to rebuild his image.

Pareja saw the situation from another point of view. This embargo was a clear lack of neutrality; such an affront was without a shadow of a doubt a full-on attack. Things took a more fortunate turn.

Particularly since two Peruvian steamers had just left the port of Valparaíso heading for Peru with Chilean volunteers and weapons aboard.

What could be said in its defence?

Nothing.

So, Pareja decided to split up his fleet. He sailed for Chile with four boats. The *Numancia* and the *Virgen* stayed off the coast of Callao, so that the Peruvians wouldn't forget that Spain was angry. And that its flag was beautiful.

Before leaving, Pareja summoned Simón.

Your reputation precedes you, he began. I hope it will follow you.

He gave Simón some paper, a handful of letters that he took out of the drawer of his writing desk. One of them was to be rewritten; it was inelegantly splotched with ink on account of the author's hesitation.

It wasn't flowing, he continued, staring at his inkwell. They tell me that you know how to fix it. You could read the previous ones as inspiration, to get the tone. That's how you say it, isn't it? The tone?

Or the style, or the voice, Simón replied, the thing that makes it you.

Pareja remained absorbed by the jet-black brilliance of the inkwell; he touched it with his finger, finally picked it up.

You will embellish, he said, make sure the effects are right and the ideas efficient. Most importantly, you won't be you.

Simón acquiesced, waited to be dismissed.

I'll pick it all up when I come back, Pareja added, because you'll stay here. You've been reassigned, Lieutenant. You're no longer attached to an orphan ship.

I have to go now. Dismissed.

⁊❧

Pareja had decided that the *Virgen* needed an additional officer, so Simón had been installed, scribe and navigator, in a cabin with no porthole, the ambiguous purpose of which – storage or dungeon – remained to be decided under the new captain. This was done unofficially, while every day more piles of fishing nets appeared around Simón's feet, as he wrote similar piles of reports. They ended up settling on a lack of accuracy they were quite comfortable with – except for Simón – in keeping with the lack of accuracy of the treaty of Tordesillas. This was no surprise; it was typical of the war to this point.

Simón was happy to hear of Pareja's departure for Chile. This would no doubt mean the relaxing of strict orders: no fraternizing with the enemy, no landing without an order to attack, no trading with the people, no setting fire to the sails.

Maybe he could try to see Montse again.

From that point on, he paced in his mind. He looked at the twinkling lights of Callao in the distance, a scattering of breadcrumbs that the fog pecked at from time to time. He sighed a great deal when the town disappeared behind the veil, and just as much when it reappeared – in other words, all the time.

Shipmates questioned him; others got him a little drunk. Simón responded that he would like to see Callao again, a pretty town, and walk through the hills. They understood immediately: everyone hated Callao, a soulless town, 'hills' an overstatement, not to mention the glaring lack of brothels.

See a young lady again, eh?

If only briefly, Simón explained.

If only to freshen up my fantasies with a bit of reality, to better imagine the shape of her eyes, the curve of her breast, you know, so that it doesn't fade away.

And who knows, they added, half joking, maybe to take things a little further.

Simón wouldn't object.

The opportunity arose quite naturally. Under the captain's tacit, unofficial approval, sailors from the *Virgen* mounted a small trading expedition. They wanted more tobacco and less vile food on board. Simón was invited to join them.

At first he hesitated. He was sleeping so well in the arms of his memories that he was afraid to leave them and dispel the dream. He used scruples as justification. I mean really, not like that, without warning. Whatever will she think?

And I don't even have flowers.

In truth, he found himself more comfortable with the idea of Montse than in her arms. He ended up being forced into the dinghy. He was a good officer, he would command the operation. He did an uncanny imitation of the Peruvian accent, which was eerie: muted tones, a practically monotonous stream of sounds, some rattling of chains on the double R – now that you mention it, it really quite suited him, or a strange double of him.

Everyone wanted to see how his story would turn out. Because the war had been boring of late. Lacking oomph, practically stalled, it left a void to fill in the men's minds. They called the other diversion to the rescue without uttering its name: lov... No, no, Simón demurred, not that serious word, barely an inclination of a few degrees.

They shoved him into the dinghy.

They told him: Of course, you're right, a little slope that's pulling you down just a bit. You have to go for it, let go, come on. We'll see if you pick up speed, Lieutenant.

꿈

It was evening. They tied the ropes to the bollard, careful not to make the knot too complicated. They might have to leave in a hurry.

Everyone was wearing dark clothes and black bandanas. Some had blackened their faces with coal. The mission started clumsily through the town. They were talking too much, discussing the supplies they needed, and their outfits were ridiculous.

The small group was cause for concern in the townspeople's homes – one of the disadvantages of the disguise, because it made them look like devil worshippers on their way to a black mass. Passersby turned; the curious pressed their noses against the windows. They would be committing their evil deeds in the hills, no doubt, or at Miss Ortuño's house. She had books that no one else would read.

The group of suspects split up to escape the vigilance of the locals. They would meet up at the home of a sympathizer who would trade provisions for a bit of gold. Except you, Lieutenant, of course, we'll see you back at the dinghy. Wink, wink, pat on the shoulder, off we go.

Simón didn't want to disappoint anyone. He set off for the Ortuño residence.

He knocked softly at the door, looked behind him, not wanting to upset the calm that was settling over the town. No one answered. He knocked again, and the maid opened the door, a bit on edge. Oh! It's you, Mr. Claro, forgive me, I thought, what you're wearing, you gave me a bit of a fright.

Simón asked her about Mademoiselle: was he disturbing her sleep, her reading, her sighing? Oh, no, not at all. Mademoiselle left for Lambayeque with her brother, who is not doing any better. He's having nightmares. And they had mentioned a trip to Tarapoto; the strong wind is good for the constitution.

Simón wanted to leave something for Montse, a token of his affection, an expression of his thoughts, to keep alive what was meant to be. He had seen it done in books. A small gift. But nothing he had with him seemed significant.

He still hadn't written a letter.

Not even any flowers.

Oh, Simón finally said. When is she coming back?

Well, Sir, well. Miss Montserrat is quite mysterious. One night you see her and the next not at all. She's like the moon.

❧

Let's get back to Pareja and his ships, which arrived in sight of Valparaíso on September 17, 1865. Three years had passed since Pinzón first took command of the fleet.

The people of Valparaíso were there, still pensive, the ocean still calm and dangerous.

Dreamers still filled the docks and women their dreams.

The mantilla had fallen out of fashion. Hair was becoming more of a distraction.

This time, however, there was more carrying on and unpleasantness than when Pinzón had come. The Spaniards were demanding apologies. The Chileans were getting annoyed by the political situation. They were kind of like the Peruvians' cousins, you know, and were even known to marry their daughters. Spain had thought Chile more respectable.

Pareja wanted to see José Joaquín Pérez, president twice over.

The meeting took place aboard the *Villa de Madrid*. Food was served. Pérez still leaned on his cane with the gold knob, and no matter what the Spaniards thought of it, was more serious than ever about his presidency of the National Ballet.

And the ballet? Pareja asked.

It's doing well, thank you, Pérez answered.

And the country?

Even better, rest assured.

Would it have been too much to ask that the Spanish fleet be welcomed with a few salutes? Say, twenty-one of them.

No, Pérez said, technically it wouldn't be a problem because, you know, Chile has more and more guns, and men to use them. Warships too, that sort of thing, coastal batteries, if you want to know. So technically no, but ethically yes.

They had a hard time understanding the Spaniards' objections. They asked for clarification. Tomorrow is the 18th, Pérez explained.

So? Pareja asked.

Well, that's the day Spain left.

They had thought it was for good. At least they had hoped.

Ignorance, Pareja said, angry. As a worthy representative of our Lord on earth, Spain has a small presence everywhere.

Well, Pérez said, it seems you're forgetting Africa, where the French are truly everywhere, for instance, and the English.

The comparison was a little shaky.

Spain always returns, Pareja went on. She is like the sun. That sort of thing.

Like certain nightmares, then.

The worst, Pareja answered.

There was anger all around. They were both ruminating, losing their appetite. Thoughts were growing confused: the veal blanquette was arrogant, Chile inedible.

What's the name of the idiot across from me again?

It's Pareja, Sir; it's Pérez, Sir – take all this away; yes, Sir.

One week later, Santiago made war official in a communiqué. It came straight to the point: scorned pride, open hostilities. Madrid was incensed. Normally we were the ones who started this sort of thing, were we not?

What do you think, Mr. O'Donnell?

Leopoldo O'Donnell, Duke of Tetuán, was the most recent new prime minister.

He didn't look Spanish, and he sported an Englishman's moustache. There was nothing refined about it, no fine tips, only big bristles, like a shoe brush, trimmed straight like a cedar hedge. Conceived in the Canary Islands fifty-six years earlier, he died two years later at Biarritz watching the wind, the stars and the sea.

He had replaced Narváez precisely over the question of Africa. His predecessor had been considered too soft and had had his head turned by the Americas to the point of getting a kink in his neck. The New World was so yesterday, after all. Spain had come, had conquered, had filled its coffers: mission accomplished.

Now it was just a matter of tending its own backyard, which, according to all evidence, was Africa. Of course, they would send a few ships to the Pacific, they would happily fight in the Andes – it was an emotional attachment. But not at the expense of the Old World, which was being rediscovered. Because their French and English neighbours were also rediscovering it, and in a hurry.

O'Donnell shared all of these ideas, and a few others as well. It pleased the court. The dark continent was in fashion, the Negro more highly regarded than the Indian. So Pareja was asked to withdraw. Forget Chile, let's finish things up on a higher note with Peru, collect a few shrimp specimens and come home.

No, Admiral Pareja replied. We cannot dishonour Spain. She is like a crazed lover. She backs down at nothing.

He was congratulated on the simile.

But all the same, hurry up and finish this war.

Not having sufficient troops to attempt a landing worthy of the name, Pareja decided to blockade the ports. It wasn't as noble, but it wasn't as expensive. Anyway, Spain had nobility to burn; she could afford to rest on her laurels. But he would have to do better than in Peru.

That was not taking into account the 2,900 kilometres of Chilean coastline.

And the Spanish ships, which were too easily counted. On one and a half hands, no more.

It was worse than in Peru.

Except in Valparaíso, where they were able to blockade the port fairly effectively. They even managed to irritate the Americans and the British, who were fond of the place. The economic losses were mounting. Formal protests were sent to Pareja, one signed by Commodore John Rodgers. Pareja didn't know him. So, to the wastebasket.

❧

Simón, who was still posted off the coast of Callao, tried thirty times to write a letter to Montse.

It was either too short or too long. It came too crudely from the heart or too coldly from the head. It wasn't perfect. So, to the wastebasket.

The *Virgen* was called in for reinforcement. A dispatch explained that the Chilean coast was longer than originally thought. A fast ship could intercept some of the more foolhardy. Peru was slug-like, in any case. And Chile, as you could see from maps, looked like a snake without end. It was shifty: no doubt this was the enemy to take down.

There were immediate manoeuvres and preparations that required the crew's attention. Simón was both relieved and disappointed that he had to stop writing.

His heart had always been divided this way. Gypsies could read his future more clearly than Simón could read his feelings.

Esmeralda: You will fall in love.

Simón: But how will I know?

He nonetheless decided to take part in the final expedition on terra firma, to gather a few supplies before sailing.

Simón held out little hope of seeing Montse again, but he wanted to return to the places they had been alone together. It would reassure him to see the same bench, a similar sidewalk. Callao couldn't have changed much. He had the sense that the lasting exteriors of the places that they had passed by retained the feeling he thought they had shared, along with the discussions, silences and looks exchanged. As long as the place remained intact, the feeling would remain intact. Better not to name it.

One year later, Verlaine would commit this animist bit of nonsense to a gloomy poem. The desire to see the sparkling waters of a port again, the endless moaning of the wind, the end of an avenue, its statue. The scent of a suitable flower. His 'After Three Years' of love that, deep in the heart, lasts an eternity.

Simón got back to serious matters. He and the men would have to row hard to reach the dock.

This time they didn't bother with disguises. The townsfolk looked on with menacing glares while merchants made deals. They chatted a little, whispered sweet nothings to the woman at the bakery, had a drink on a terrace. Then they loaded the supplies into the dinghes.

As they were doing all this, Simón saw a familiar silhouette. She was coming down from the town, bouncing from one passerby to the next, from one stall to the next.

It was the Ortuño maid, who stopped to scold the nephew and give him another life lesson. He was into marbles now. He was grow-ing up.

Simón waved to her. She recognized him: Mademoiselle has returned!

When? Simón asked, knocking over a bottle of wine.

The bottle was too dusty, or too slippery, of course. A stray cat lapped up the liquid, its caramel fur speckled with spatters.

Yesterday, Sir; she's still asleep.

Is she getting better? Is she smiling more?

No more, no less, the maid said. Mademoiselle dropped from fatigue when she arrived. She kept muttering.

Simón didn't dare ask what.

Is she dreaming a lot?

You know, Mademoiselle is always off somewhere, never in the here and now. She dreams standing up.

Simón was tempted to go fetch her in her dreams. But duty called, time was of the essence. And there was something else: a semblance of pride. Hadn't she decided – with no goodbyes, not a moment's hesitation – to leave for Lambayeque after they met?

Why couldn't he do likewise?

Why didn't he have her strength and detachment?

Maybe that was actually what she wanted him to do. To prove how similar they were, to show her that they were cut from the same strong cloth, made to understand one another, a kindred spirit in freedom and independence. Leaving would bring them closer together.

Time to go, said Simón. It's nice to see you again, but I have to go.

He explained that war awaited him. He was even moved himself. It was all heroism: duty, courage, stoicism. He wished Montse could have been there to hear him. She would have begged him to stay. Obviously, he would have had to say no, to stay in character.

What should I tell Mademoiselle? The maid was concerned.

She was afraid of a misstep, without knowing what it could be, of letting an opportunity slip by. Maybe her mistress would be disappointed that she failed to keep the lieutenant from leaving.

She will ask questions, you know. It would be better if I said nothing of you being here.

No, Simón answered, tell her what I said. And to explain my departure, you can simply add that ...

He looked off in the distance.

One day I burn bright, blazing ...

He closed his eyes.

... and the next day I am gone, obscured by the clouds.

Like the sun.

But Sir, the maid insisted, you could come with me; there is the vestibule, and it will probably only take a minute, and ...

No, Simón interrupted her. The sun doesn't control the clouds.

And he was off. Proud of himself.

11

Too much sea dulls the mind. Still more sea torments it. It's the surface of the water that does it; at first hypnotic and all-consuming, it soon becomes a blank sheet on which you are meant to write the rest of your life. A dulled mind starts to daydream, and then is anxious about standing still.

For days Simón had been pacing the cabins, the holds and the decks. He sought out any conversation he could find to calm his nerves. He would stop to talk about the size of rations or a weakening mast. He revived dying conversations with important philosophical matters and comments on worm holes in the hull. It all depended on the intelligence of the person he was talking to, which didn't necessarily reflect rank.

The fact was that he had grown unsure about his decision in Callao, made under the pretense of independence. He was tormented to the point that he could no longer write his reports, let alone a letter to Montse. It wasn't for want of thinking about it. He thought of nothing but her. She was in every allusion to Callao, to Spain, to women in general, to umbrellas in particular, to anything. It was as though all of his thoughts had her hair wrapped around them. And his fixation could be displaced only in brief moments of relief: urination, sleep, danger.

Once calm was restored in the world, the storm would start to rage inside him.

They had been sailing in the direction of Chile and Pareja for many days. The *Virgen* had passed Coquimbo and would soon arrive within sight of Valparaíso. November was November. The sky was drained of colour; the seas were growing rougher. Determined waves licked the sailors' ankles, reaching almost as high as their morale, which was low.

Simón had been daydreaming on his bunk since morning. Montse was lying on top of him, lying next to him, lying underneath him, lying under the bed, any form of lying that would allow for any sort of caress. This had been going on for two long hours – his imagination was starting to flag – when the alert sounded.

Montse disappeared into the shape of the sheets, and Simón was able to get up.

On deck, it was explained that a ship flying an English flag was approaching. It was the *Esmeralda*, a corvette. Not a very English name, of course, because it was in fact Chilean. But it had taken the Spaniards some time to unmask the imposter. The first clue was the *Esmeralda* releasing a small, powdery, quickly dissipated cloud from its side, like a puff from a pipe. A geyser of foam followed, a sort of spray of pale wheat immediately carried off by the wind.

The ship wished us harm.

Of course, they asked for an explanation for the fistful of white sand released into the wind before moving on. The explanation took the form of slivers embedded in the calves of the sailors, and wood shards driven into the base of the masts. Three men who were hit cried out in pain and in unison, although at times taking turns, producing a sort of continuous cry barely modulated by the tone of their voices, suggesting that suffering can be more unifying than a conductor. The port side of the *Virgen* now had an asymmetrical hole, a clear, unsightly message.

They wished the ship harm in return.

The ship finally decided to come clean. They had dragged their feet aboard the *Esmeralda*, taking their time to find the proper flag; the slow pace made it seem ceremonial. Or perhaps they had been dishonest, slow to admit that they would have to make it official after all, to show remorse. No matter. In Callao, the Spaniards had talked to the Peruvians, the Peruvians to the Chileans. They had discovered the itinerary of the *Virgen*. They had been expecting it. They would sink it.

They got the battle they had been looking for. The *Virgen* extended its cannons. They were lined up along its side like decaying teeth. They countered the attack, subtracting a few Chileans, although mainly adding new waves to the sea. The *Virgen*'s cannons weren't rusty, but its artillerymen were.

Simón ran. He tried to help the injured and buoy the spirits of the despairing. A bit of blood spattered the sails and his hands, got lodged under his nails; that would be harder to clean. Spain's aim wasn't very good. It was firing like an old man coughing: no consistency, no power. They were missing the enemy a great deal given how little they were firing.

The captain gave the order to cease fire. The *Virgen* was having a hard time responding. Gunfire had taken chunks out of its masts. The holds were swallowing fish. It was like a casualty clawing its way through the sea, and behind it, the long stream of debris was its entrails.

The *Esmeralda* was soon at its side. The two ships were so close that it was as if one were holding the other up. The order was given to board the ship. The *Virgen*'s crew surrendered as a matter of course. A battle with cannons was all well and good, but fighting like pirates, no thank you. The Chilean engineers tried to save the ship. They would take it over; they would take good care of it. They took as prisoners 115 sailors, whom they would take less good care of. And six officers, whom they would treat decently.

Simón was one of them. He was ordered to hand over all of his papers. These included part of Pareja's correspondence; Simón had prettied it up with a few rewrites and embellishments. The writing was flowery, the writing of love letters. It was over.

❧

The prisoners were brought to Valparaíso.

After negotiations, the Spanish ships blocking the port gave passage to the *Esmeralda*, which honourably unloaded the captives and would leave the harbour again only at its risk and peril. The Chileans had also promised good conditions for the officers' detention: meals served with wine and, in the cells, if possible, a window that looked out onto something other than a wall. The others would get whatever could be found.

The Spaniards had promised not to fire as they went by, nothing more.

That was already something, given the humiliation, the insult, Isabelle's coming wrath. It was noble of them not to send the Esmeralda to the bottom of the sea, thought a ruminating Pareja, who was watching the Chilean ship go by from aboard the *Villa de Madrid*. That coconut shell was laughing at Spain. Spain would crush it.

Pareja's annoyance was interrupted by a mail petty officer who had come to announce the prisoner count and the names of the officers. The admiral seemed worried once Lieutenant Claro was mentioned. Had any papers had been taken from him?

Your Excellency's personal correspondence, Your Excellency.

Very well, dismissed. Come back here.

Close the door at least.

Pareja paced the deck, his head bowed, all night. He didn't return the sailors' salutes, contemplating his future and his boots more than his troops. Then he stopped for a moment near the main mast and stroked it gently before returning to his quarters.

Once there, he wrote a note. He put on his best uniform, with frogging and buttons on the cuff carved with manticores, with roller coasters at the wrists. He lay down on his bed. He loaded his revolver, thought to himself that he really didn't want to go through with it – but the others would suggest it. As much to avoid their looks, the viscountess's disgrace, her husband's face turning red, the general discomfort in the court, he put a bullet in his brain. The pillow was livid, turned red, soaked up the blood until its thirst was quenched and – it was a lot of fluid – spilled a little onto the bedding, which in turn saturated the Persian carpet. The carpet was burgundy, so the blood blended in, and to the innocent observer it added two or three patterns at the most. The stains would hardly show.

Pareja's eyes stayed open. They were calm and yet haunted by reflections. Valparaíso; the sea; you, dear reader. Like fossils or sediment, memories seemed to have been deposited in them, minuscule speckles in the pupil like the last bubbles released by a drowning man.

His parting note read that honour demanded suicide. His final wish was to be buried at sea, but for pity's sake, not in Chilean waters. Adieu.

After the *Triunfo* was sunk by the seagulls, the *Virgen* had fallen into enemy hands, and Pareja had committed suicide, it was clear that the war was a serious affair. There were whispers in Madrid that the admiral's correspondence had contained intimate details. Smutty fakes circulated; they were in hot demand. The war was finally heating up.

It had also driven Pezet from power in Peru. It had hurt the Chilean economy and the pride of the president of the National Ballet. It had irritated the Americans and the British. They still had their eye on the Spanish fleet. They were patrolling the surrounding waters and diplomatic corridors. They were looking disapprovingly at Isabelle II.

And yet of all of these players, none were concerned about the fate of Simón, who had fallen into enemy hands, except for the enemy himself, who took the time to find him an adequate cell where he could rot, and you, dear reader, of course, concerned about his fate, worried about his loneliness, to the point that you are willing to rot with him for a while – but only a while, because you will escape.

Here's how.

Núñez

1865–1866

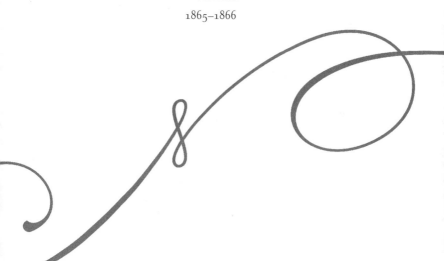

12

Simón disembarked in Valparaíso. As an officer, he was entitled to smiles from the young ladies. He was able to keep his gold pen and was even given a window. In the longest moments of the day, he held the former between his fingers, sitting before the latter. He wrote four lines of a journal, hunched over a tiny desk, and wore himself out. Then he found his motivation: this would sell in Madrid, where tales of prisoners sent the duchesses into a tizzy.

In between vainglorious daydreams, he watched the city through the window and tried to remember his walks. He hardly recognized the streets he had wandered. He got tired of writing badly and reliving nothing, and asked for some newspapers. Some of them were unreadable. Others reported on the progress of the war and a rancher's wedding, where the best sires were on show, because the bovine world never sleeps. As far as the war went, the Spanish fleet had a new admiral, Casto Méndez Núñez. He didn't have a moustache, but he had full sideburns that he regularly scratched, both when he was thinking and when he wasn't. He was credited with ideas of coastal bombardments and Galician superiority. He would have to succeed where his predecessors Pinzón and Pareja had failed. Striking harder summed up his strategy. He dreamed of a statue in Madrid, Plaza de Cibeles.

Simón wanted to meet him. Another character for his writing, perhaps. Stature, nerve, ego, all suggestive of genius. Or potential for deception. We shall see.

But to meet the strange character, he would first have to escape from Valparaíso. Opportunities to run off – already limited in Simón's optimistic flights of fancy – were near zero once he came back down to the ground. Crossing a footbridge during exercise time, he could catch a glimpse over the walls of the fleet's masts pitching; an optical illusion turned the barbed wire and the parapets into sails. But soon a branch or a cloud would restore perspective – creating a sad, distant realm – and dash hope.

Simón observed, analyzed and questioned his jailer, who doubled as a manservant. A banal name, Ramón, for an average, disappointed man,. They ended up fraternizing: I would love to visit Madrid. The city is overrated. My wife is mad at me. It's far worse to be alone. Once they patted each other on the shoulder. Simón wound up telling him his story: their meeting, the war being waged and his own smaller skirmish. Ramón felt sorry for him. He was reminded of the romance he never had, but that he had dreamed of from age twelve to sixteen. Most men expect someone else to act for them in areas where they lack expertise, be it politics, or clock-making, or love. Ramón felt he was finally getting his chance, by proxy, to express his emotions and – in a flight of fancy – to write. So he found some paper. Write that letter, go on – I'll make sure it gets to her. Simón hesitated. Confinement makes you soft, and to keep stirring up all these feelings? No, such melancholy. I mean, it's not as though we're orphans.

Ramón swore he wouldn't say another word until Simón had written the letter right in front of him, and signed it, and polished it. As polished as the lady you describe.

Were her nipples really so hard they could make a sword quiver?

So Simón withdrew inside himself for a few days. He tried to find a letter in there. He had to look higher, lower, in the middle of his chest. He wanted to express his feelings. To find the exact, singular words that Montse would understand. He sweated over it. Since the future was uncertain – what with prison, the war and Ramón's good will – Simón wanted to promise nothing, hope for little and express only his feelings stripped bare of fiction.

In short, he wanted to add words to his silences in Callao.

But he went back and forth between what he wanted to do and fawning: I put my arm around your waist, I long for your mouth, you smell like exotic flowers. He wanted the impossible, a raft. He said too much, your ankle. He crossed out words.

Then one evening when he was thinking back to the theatre, the menu, their walk and Montse's hair, it all came together. He got up to put down on paper the words that were jostling around inside him, but as if in slow motion, clear and right and soft as slow tears that the eye lets fall after they have rested a time on the eyelashes.

It was a short, simple letter. A beautiful letter. It said what men couldn't manage to say – women either, as a matter of fact. Not you. Not me.

13

Simón learned the fine art of waiting. Since writing the letter, he had found new ways of twiddling his thumbs: clockwise, counter-clockwise, alternating, revolutionary. Hope was his only true escape.

Ramón had promised to come up with a plan. Something safe. Night watchmen lingering over a cigarette near the west wall, a sergeant passed out from too much wine at nine o'clock, a small boat in the port to reach the Spanish fleet. And for the road, cookies made by his wife. Something comforting.

But the smell of the cookies always ended up waking the sergeant or attracting the smokers. Conversations dragged on. Oh, how lucky to have a wife, damn Ramonito and his epicurean ways, and before you knew it Simón was asleep in his cell. The cigarette break was over. They would wait until tomorrow, next week and, without saying it, for destiny to point the way.

❧

It did more than just point. The Chilean government first gave them the finger by refusing to open its ports to ships from neutral nations having dealings with the Spaniards. Spain gave the finger back; Chilean policy was completely insane.

What an insult! Núñez cried. It's like a child not playing fair. We will burn Valparaíso to the ground. We will bombard them, you'll see. Come come, the Americans weighed in, let's try to stay calm, come on, let's not get carried away. War goes where it will, Núñez said at last.

Spain didn't have to ask for Chile's hand in marriage, but a modicum of restraint, diplomacy oblige. At the very least, Hugh Judson Kilpatrick, Washington's ambassador to Chile, insisted, let's not destroy an entire city.

All I see is a village, Núñez replied.

Realizing that Spain would not back down, Kilpatrick asked the captain of the American fleet opportunely anchored in the port to threaten the Spaniard. His name was John Rodgers.

Listen, Mr. Núñez, it's nothing personal. It's just that we're trading and …

Enough, interrupted Núñez, who was no more familiar with him than with Boston. I will be forced to sink the American ships. And even if we have only one ship left afloat, I will bombard Valparaíso.

He added that he and the queen preferred honour and no ships to ships and no honour. It was his sound bite for the history books.

A little bird told Simón that the wings of destiny would soon help him sweep aside the prison walls – or at least the newspapers did.

❧

The destruction of Valparaíso began on January 31, 1866. Ecuador had declared war on Spain the night before. Simón read about it in a dispatch. The article, between patriotic outcry and a call for an alliance among South American republics, didn't explain the reasons for the decision very clearly. But Simón knew that Admiral Núñez would waste no time in responding.

Night fell on the squares, streets and houses. Then shells fell on them. The Chilean merchant fleet, anchored in the port, was destroyed. Whistler, on board an American ship, had just painted it the evening before, thinking that Ecuador joining the war wouldn't change anything, reflecting that, all the same, the merchant fleet was exposed in the extreme, and he added a lantern here, a mast there – a little masterpiece in ochre and blue that depicted the frightened shadows of the ships quivering in the water.

Ramón was complaining. Running was no longer his forte, even less so zigzagging under exploding projectiles. He announced that a section of the west wall had fallen, that there would be rocks to climb and the half-buried limbs of two or three guards to look away from. The boat waited near the worm-eaten wooden dock in the port. Worm-eaten wood, you say, not worm-eaten iron or stone. And don't forget the letter; keep it close to your heart.

Thank you, Ramón, I won't forget.

Good. Just tell your artillerymen comrades to spare my house.

And he unlocked the cell.

Here's a pistol, just in case.

They walked, playing the part of guard and prisoner. They crossed the long yard. Cannons and guns powdered the night. Once they arrived at the opening in the west wall, they discreetly shook hands.

That's where their friendship ended.

Simón ran toward the port. Even more than the shells, he had to avoid people seeking refuge outside the city. Women were crying. Husbands were calming them by slapping them across the face. A few dead were lying primly on the ground. Their faces couldn't be seen, nor could their blood. They were positioned neither too close together nor too far apart, sustaining the distress: a body appeared just as the last one was forgotten. They all looked alike.

In fact, it could have been the same extra who, once Simón passed, got up and ran, taking a shortcut and lying down further along his path. A question of budget.

Simón finally reached an alley that sloped down toward the ships. Behind him, the bombardments hung butterflies of flames in the far-off hills. They were growing in number, calling out to one other, the first acting as a beacon to the rest, which quickly settled around it.

At the end of the alley were two smiling eyes. A child was playing with a dead dog. The guts formed the roads and the teeth made the mountains. Simón didn't dare shoo the child away for fear of alerting the Chilean troops. He rushed into a dangerous back alley that he thought would lead to the port's square. He looked back once. The child had discovered the body of a man. The eyes formed the ponds.

Simón finally reached the docks. Ahead of him the scene had changed to one of amputated masts and eviscerated hulls. The Chilean merchant fleet seemed clenched in pain, and the moon, which was full, seemed delighted. From the distant sea rose puffs of smoke as if from pipes, floating up in compact white balloons, which dissipated slowly, finally dying on the spindles of stars. Spain was shelling to its heart's content.

There is poetry to this war, Simón thought. It will last. As long as art can be created from it, it will last. And he took another look at the painting come to life. The fleet was a little too far off, a bit diffuse in the smoke. He would have changed the composition, if only to save him squinting, and rowing. My arms are already sore. Art should at least be accessible.

The decrepit dock was guarded by two sailors whose wrinkles made them twins. They had been handed weapons and given orders to let no one sail. They were afraid of spies escaping – I mean, sure why not – or panicked citizens giving themselves up to the enemy. Keep an eye peeled, gentlemen. Indeed one of them had only one left.

Simón approached with the stealth of a storybook assassin: hugging the walls, disappearing in the shadows. Once he arrived near an empty stall that smelled like fish, he loaded his pistol.

He wondered how he would reach the boat. He wondered how he would get around the men and other similar things. How was it possible for a stall to stink this much?

He wouldn't be able to hide out there for very long.

A projectile crashed headlong into the port square. The Spanish ballistic strategy consisted of sweeping the city, starting with the peaks and ending with the toes. In fact, they decided to tickle them (a second shell hit a pile of rowboats) and keep tickling until it turned to pain (a flowerbed took a third hit), until no one was laughing anymore.

Simón had to do something.

He got up and pointed his gun at the sailors. Still reeling from the bombardment, they didn't take the overture very well. And yet it was fairly conventional, and they should have understood it instinctively. Weapons dropped for lives spared. Those words in a different order.

Thinking instead that it was a landing, the sailors raised their weapons. The words *swine* and *Spaniard* were heard and then they started firing. They missed Simón, putting holes in the stall. They did their best to camouflage themselves behind large fishing nets to reload. One of their heads stuck out above a cable and another's ass from behind a barrel.

Simón thought about life and death, his and theirs. He wanted to see Montse again, and time was of the essence. Troops had been alerted. A shell had just landed in the alley where the child was. The child.

Since the child was probably buried under the rubble, nothing mattered anymore. Certainly not the lives of the two old men shooting at him. The child's death excused the rest, veiling any crime behind a darker injustice that would obliterate the rest of it, Valparaíso, Peru, everything, his hopes, everything again, his love – well, almost everything.

Simón rushed the old men who were still reloading their weapons, tearing the cartridges from each others' hands, explaining to each other how to do it. Simón positioned himself behind the first one, killing him with a bullet to the head. The second one looked at him with his one black eye. Fear had hung a wet star in it.

He should have begged for mercy; instead, he took his knife out of his old boot. Instinct kills as many as it saves. Simón stuck his pistol in the hollow of the dark pupil. There was very little kickback. The eyes became symmetrical, two craters, one smoking, the other already extinguished. The body dropped onto the nets.

Simón quickly found the boat Ramón had prepared; cookies wrapped in a newspaper was the confirmation. He rowed at a steady pace. Once past the remains of the Chilean fleet and a few bodies impeding his progress, he let the surf rock him and nibbled on a cookie. He rested. His head was killing him.

He asked himself whether he had killed for a woman.

Basically, he believed, people always kill for a love somewhere.

To see people again.

14

Simón's explanations kept being interrupted by explosions; between cannonballs, he managed to make it understood that he was a lieutenant. He was hoisted aboard the *Villa de Madrid*, then left to his own devices. They would bring him to the captain soon, after the operation. The captain was occupied with his spyglass and adjusting aim, you see.

Simón roamed the deck a little. His aching muscles limited his journey to as far as the nearest crate; he sat down. The lack of sleep was making him hallucinate an opera set: ropes, smoke, sails and stars. The cannons were the tenors, the whistling projectiles the sopranos. Sailors were walking around fearlessly, taking over from one another on cards and cannons. They knew that they were the only ones singing. Valparaíso, defenceless, stage right, was silent.

The Spanish solo continued. It was knocking the city senseless, and it was slumping like a tired spectator. Simón leaned his elbows on the ship's railing, curious. He saw that Valparaíso on fire was no more than rippling gash, like bright lips in the night.

A pale stroke of light under a large black door.

That sort of thing.

Something to keep the artists busy.

⁊

The pointlessness of it! Núñez was fuming. A small, insignificant village like Valparaíso. Once the merchant fleet was condemned to the depths, there was nothing more strategic about this attack. They were sending a message, of course, they had been repeating it for hours; the Chileans had probably understood it by now or had had their eardrums split.

Núñez scratched his sideburns. He had to think.

He gave the order to cease fire.

He shut himself in his cabin.

Pinzón had hit the economy in vain – the economy was the arm – and he had hit the population – the population was the legs. The thing was to hit the heart.

Yet it was a naval battle, and ships were what would carry the day. The navy would be the sinews; victory would be found on the sea. They had to beat the enemy in naval combat. Once vanquished, it would retreat to a few strongholds and look out at an ocean now out of reach. The ships of the Spanish armada would dot the water like ominous little islands in motion. Like a barrier reef on which their boats would sink. So there could be no world without Spain. And then he would restore the honour Pareja had lost.

As a matter of fact, Núñez thought, an allied fleet was approaching. Spies and natives had told him. Its ships were anchored in the Chiloé Archipelago, alongside Abtao Island. Five ships, one of them an old friend: the *Virgen de Covadonga*, captured by the enemy. An attack, victory, Peruvians swimming with the fishes. A statue, one can only hope.

Núñez went out on deck. He breathed, in long inhales, held his breath, waiting till he had to exhale. That felt better. Morning was breaking. He didn't want to think anymore. He scratched his sideburns. In the air, he could hear Valparaíso crackling and warming the entire bay. The clouds looked like marshmallows.

∿

The natives hadn't lied.

The new president of Peru, Mariano Ignacio Prado, was trying to prove that he was a man of action rather than contemplation. They had applauded his investiture speech: unlike his predecessor

Pezet, the only theatre he would care about would be the theatre of operations.

He had immediately ordered the frigates *Apurímac* and *Amazonas* to head to Abtao Island. They were to join the corvettes *Unión* and *América* and then attack the Spanish fleet. They wanted to engage the enemy, someone to blame, results. They wanted people dancing in the streets.

A schooner, until recently Chilean, the *Virgen de Covadonga*, would escort them. The ship still hadn't been to the Philippines or seen any mail.

But there was a bit of a setback: the currents dashed the *Amazonas* against a rock and eviscerated her. This was followed by a ballet of men in the water, between the planks, their bodies drifting, their legs rippling like mops and their arms clutching barrels: like a painting by Géricault.

They feared the octopus below, with its poisonous suction cups, the strange bird-like beak, the ink that Satan writes with. They had to force themselves to think of what the barrels could hold: wine, fresh water, a stowaway. Then they kept their minds busy with a *Pater Noster* or a *Hail Mary*.

Quite a few were fished out of the water, and the rest were officially missing, giving their families hope that they were spending a dream life on a desert island or were rescued by mermaids.

Although they were sinking their own ships and others were being stolen from them, the Spaniards were at least trying to avoid the reefs. The *Villa de Madrid* and *Reina Blanca* successfully kept their course and sighted Abtao on February 7, 1866. As a result of his new ambition, Núñez had given the order to break up the blockade of Valparaíso and go say hello.

They entered the strait beyond which the allied fleet was anchored. The fleet politely came to meet them. A lot of numbers followed.

Spain opened fire at three in the afternoon, trying to reach the enemy over 1,600 metres away. The Peruvian/Chilean fleet returned fire. With surprising precision, it almost hit the Castilian hulls. The renegade *Virgen de Covadonga* (Chile) even hit the *Reina Blanca* (Spain) over 600 metres away. It was Spanish built, the Spaniards explained, hence its performance and good looks. They didn't pay any attention to Simón, who pointed out its ineffective firing at point-blank range during the battle of Papudo. Cannonballs that couldn't hit an elephant.

That was a case of bad weather, my dear man. Grey on grey, you know. Whereas today the sun casts a shadow.

Whatever.

Finally two lines of ships squared off against each other. The Spanish line was rather short. They saluted the intention. They fired. The ships eventually dispersed and filled with smoke. They looked like floating cauliflowers. They spun around, sped up and slowed down, formed and reformed pairs. The North Wind was the gentleman dancer's arms. They searched for it to get back in step. The small ships had white skirts of sails and smoke over their heads. At around five o'clock, drunk from the wind, no one really knew what they were doing anymore.

There were still results. The *Apurímac* (Peru) was hit repeatedly below its waterline and had to retreat. The *América* and the *Unión* (Peru and Peru) were each hit once. Two men died: a recruit and a cook. But the *Villa de Madrid* and the *Reina Blanca* (Spain and Spain) were the big winners, receiving eleven and sixteen cannonballs respectively (Peru and Peru).

One thousand five hundred shots were exchanged, and then the two Spanish frigates bowed out of the dance. It was because of the shoals and the fatigue. It had been nice, violent, a satisfying battle in the heart of the bay, a respectable show. Finally a real war was coming together, with the numbers to back it up.

Simón was still alive.

His hands were proof that the battle had indeed taken place: the joints were black and there were scratches on his palms. The blood under his nails would be hard to remove, as everyone knows. It didn't matter, though, because he thought he had lost the letter. Three times he patted his inside pocket to reassure himself and, at the end, when all of his senses were dazed, he took it out to look at it. Combat had improved it: the sea water added tears, blood added kisses. The letter had lost some of its machismo, and yet, given the causes – the emotion, the war – the effect had remained intact.

Both sides were waiting for reinforcements from home. Both sides tried to intercept the enemy's reinforcements. The ships floated at a distance, watching. The sailors didn't do much of anything. Clean the decks, report to the admirals.

Think of Montse, whose face was becoming a mere spectre.

Simón searched his memory, which was increasingly filled with cannons, elephants, skirts – Montse.

Sometimes he saw her between two waves, a sort of apparition floating on the surface of the water with hair of algae. Talk to me, sing. But she moved silently, her image broke apart, disappeared in a waltz of sails.

Sometimes it was just a seagull.

15

Núñez scratched his sideburns with his left hand, then with his right. His pipe moved from his lips to the fingers of each hand in turn. Then a thought came to him that broke the pattern: the pipe was put down.

He was disappointed at having caused so little destruction.

The bombardment of Valparaíso had been an insipid exercise in style, the battle of Abtao a disappointing mazurka. Then he had personally headed toward the archipelago with the *Numancia*, the *Resolución* and other ships to force a decisive battle, but the allies had refused him. They feared his panache, to say nothing of his sideburns. Who could blame them?

Then there had been a bit of hide and seek, some skirmishes, an interception here, reinforcements there, a Chilean ship (*Pampero*) captured by a Spanish ship (*Gerona*), to even the score. And so it went, passing each other on the Pacific, staging ambushes in the inlets, growing flotillas into fleets, with the ultimate goal of forming an armada that would finish off the dance partner for good. After three months of this far-off goal, Núñez was coming to a conclusion: what this conflict lacked was decisive action – action that would result in a laying down of arms and flags captured.

Núñez stared across the room at a chart that could no longer be seen through the smoke and the crude markings. The outlines of the Americas with no national borders, names of oceans without a legend, arrows related to possible operations disappearing behind a grey veil that created a brand new war. That's it, Núñez said to himself, we have to start over.

Nothing had happened yet: no victory, no defeat, their hulls were still virtually intact, because of the previous admirals' fear of a misstep that would cost them Isabelle's favour. They had sidestepped, taken the enemy from behind, studied the situation, tried to preserve their meagre force, not realizing that with every dispatch, it was expanding by a few ships.

It had casually become the largest fleet ever assembled in South American waters: fourteen ships and 250 souls. Assembled might be an overstatement, because the different operations had it scattered along a ridiculously long coast. Spain had been entranced by the Chilean serpent.

Núñez scratched both sideburns at once.

All he had to do was to concentrate this force into a single closed fist and strike the enemy a fatal blow on its largest protuberance. A clout fairly played, however, militarily speaking, so that the European newspapers couldn't question the legitimacy of the Spanish victory. It was like a fight between rams – did they ever attack from behind?

In a fit of passion, he invoked Corneille.

Once the invocation was over, the smoke dissipated and an omen appeared. Núñez could make out the city of Callao on the chart.

Destroying it would be just the thing:

1. TIt was an adequately defended fortress.
2. It was the largest port in Peru.
3. The location that wasn't all that ugly – landscape artists could do something with it.
   For example:
3a. the city's ruins; 3b. me posing at the bow of the ship; 3c. the sfumato of the background, and all that.
   I could be touching a leper. Why not?

Núñez picked up his pipe again.

The next time, he swore, the smoke would be from the cannons.

The weeks trickled by in days of fog, days of overcast skies, the sun coming out occasionally to create the impression of holidays.

Most of the allied fleet waited off the coast of Chile for reinforcements from other places. Then they would track the coast north to engage the enemy.

The Spanish fleet was slowly assembling not far from Callao.

Soon they would head toward the port, where they would start the bombardment and force a confrontation. They would have to pick up the pace, because the Peruvian-Chilean-Ecuadorian fleet, while still unclear as to its official designation, was increasingly a force to be reckoned with.

Indeed, on March 22, 1866, Bolivia joined the ball. At that point it still had access to the sea and could play with its ships elsewhere than on Poopó Lake. It would kick itself for supporting Chile a few years later during the War of the Pacific (1879–1884), when the very same Chile would be its enemy. The stakes would no longer be shit and Spain, but rather saltpetre and British influence. It would lose a province, a good deal of pride, and it would look back with yearning at the no longer existent possibility of an alliance, a few years earlier, with Madrid.

As for Brazil, Argentina and Uruguay, they had given their final refusal to join in on the affair at the end of March. It was because they were already occupied with their own war with Paraguay. The conflict, forged without the help of the Europeans and waged just as independently, was over industrial jealousy and a mad dictator: Francisco Solano López, a fan of both Prussia and Napoleon III.

The embassies offered their excuses: you understand, of course, that there is nothing encouraging happening on the battlefield that would prompt us to get involved. The conflict was in its early days, the enemy forces were well matched, Asunción was harbouring a despot. Still, it was moving to see a continent united against a former colonial power. So they would see what they could do, in a few years, if Spain still hadn't left.

We'll keep you in mind.

The *Villa de Madrid* was still afloat. Its sails had a few scars, and its hull showed signs of a squabble or two. Simón shut himself in his new cabin, which reminded him of his old one, a small closet filled with barrels and rigging. He was not reading, not writing, not eating. He was worrying. Engaging Abtao was no longer in the cards after Núñez's arrival; they were headed to Callao. There was talk of destroying the city.

A nice little project for Spain, but Simón was worried that his love would be harmed in the process. He thought of Montse sleeping, the bombardments. Montse frightened, the pillaging. Montse under rubble, certain parts of her body crushed, necessarily the most delicate parts under the least delicate rocks.

He checked the condition of the letter and the integrity of its seal once more.

He wondered whether she thought of him – if they were thinking of each other. Will she contact me? Does she want me to contact her? Should I have deserted? Now they might die. Love was becoming less amusing. Once the mystery and the naiveté are gone, all that remains is the torment.

16

On April 25, 1866, Simón and Núñez finally sighted Callao. For a while, fog shrouded the cannons newly decorating the city. Then they gradually appeared, eyes of wildcats lit up by the night around the camp, or in this case the metaphor turned on its head: daylight around the water, the black eyes rather than light. Eyes of creatures that curse you.

Callao awaited. Many pairs of eyes looked on from relatively few windows. They were fixed first on the Spanish fleet, which, in V formation, with the small ships at the back, made for a dramatic approach, but they also looked at the streets below, where troops and militias now fidgeted, galvanized into action by President Prado. They shored up the barricades and hauled additional batteries up into the hills near the strongholds, taking advantage of the tatters of fog to hide their movements.

The mayor was holding forth about past exploits: that time when they had driven back Francis Drake, that other time when John Hawkins had waved the white flag, that time when …

Standing on a case of shells in front of city hall, he explained to the small but courageous crowd that they had Armstrongs and Blakelys, revolutionary cannons that were monuments to the genius of the human mind. They had arranged them in two armoured batteries, Junín and La Merced. Of course, they would do maximum damage to the enemy. They could start whetting their pride.

They also had ships (*Colón, Tumbes, Sachaca*), along with confederate-style ships with rams (*Loa, Victoria*), all currently in harbour. They were just waiting for Spain to attack to set sail and respond. And of course troops were positioned here, and there, and there. He pointed.

A sergeant and three men came running. The bayonets pointed the way home to the crowd, and then they grabbed the mayor. He was talking too much, there were spies hiding behind the curtains, plants and cases of shells. He was congratulated for his war effort, but that would do. They took him to his beige and brown office at city hall, where he looked at the round portrait, and it moved him. His wife and his son had already left for a safer location. Would he ever see them again?

He smoked.

The Spanish fleet tried to study the Peruvian positions through the fog and the distance. Once the charts were sufficiently filled in, they entered the Bay of Callao. It was May 2. The battle had begun.

Simón had come up with a plan:

1. The *Villa de Madrid* was approaching the coast to engage the enemy in combat.
2. Simón would reach said coast aboard a second vessel.
3. He would get to Montse and deliver his letter.
4. They would share a sweet kiss.

Of course Simón had first convinced the captain of the *Villa* to let him mount a sabotage expedition involving sailors as disreputable as in the times of illicit Peruvian-Spanish trade, with camouflages just as discreet, and a few minuscule dinghies. The captain was immediately won over by this strategic fantasy. Admiral Núñez would be impressed later, perhaps there would even be a few decorations – he would encourage Claro. Particularly given that the lieutenant was familiar with the city, its underground networks, its shifty characters, the lady at the bakery.

But keep the raping to a minimum.

The plan may have appeared laughably simple, but the official cover of fearlessness gave it some chance of success. They would have no problem reaching the coast, and since everything had been approved by the captain, they avoided the bother of theft and desertion. Simón would then cleverly get lost in the chaos of combat, for which a heroic 'leave me here, I'll catch up' should suffice.

Only a few of the men accompanying him suspected the true reason for the expedition. Simón had spoken too often of a women in recent days, taking advantage of the camaraderie that had developed between them. This required of them their silent support. They were going along essentially to help Simón in his adventure and maybe to find out how it ended, or how it began. His deception didn't bother them; they were romantics. They thought of the Spanish women, with their tears and their handkerchiefs, left behind on the docks of Cadix. The rest of the men thought more about Peruvian women, about the rape that didn't bother them any more than the deception bothered the others, when you came right down to it.

The Spanish fleet split in two: one assault group headed to the north of the bay, a second to the south. At twelve fifteen, Núñez gave the order to the *Numancia*, part of the northern group, to fire on the Santa Rosa fortifications. The order was executed, and fire was returned. The ship and the little fort put on a show for ten minutes, and then the entire watch of the Numancia was reduced to silence by an accurately aimed shell. Come about, yelled Núñez, come about!

He scratched his sideburns nervously.

While they tried to manoeuvre, a second projectile hit the Numancia. Núñez was not spared. An itching sensation started in his leg, and then the blood stained his pants.

Look, my shirt too.

The admiral was wounded. One side stopped firing, then the other, out of growing curiosity. The concern lasted fifteen minutes. Núñez made sure that everything was okay – minor scrapes resulting from two or three shards, come on, get up. He mopped a little sweat, and then the cannonfire again, sideburns again, everyone was reassured.

Ordering his men to row harder still, Simón looked on the ceasefire as bad news. The lull could allow for Peruvian vigilance to shift to the south side of the bay. They would spot the *Villa de Madrid*, and then – what's that? – an enemy dinghy floating a little beyond it. They would suspect a reconnaissance mission, a landing, a diversion – certainly not a futile desire to reach one's soulmate. A cannon would be adjusted, a dispatch sent to the coastal patrols, and that's the way love would end: with weapons.

When the *Numancia* resumed firing a few minutes later, Simón was relieved that they were getting back to the business of killing each other. They would have other things to do than to adjust cannons by so much as an inch or even to send a dispatch.

And so it was.

A Blakely cannon was silenced. Then a Spanish shell crushed the La Merced battery, killing its entire crew with one strike. Twisted iron created a column of black smoke and a lot of coughing. One of those coughing was the Peruvian Secretary of Defence, José Gálvez. The troops yelled to the heroes, and the clamour shored up the Peruvians' courage.

The future of the battle was looking bright.

It's going so well, Simón thought.

The dinghy reached the shore. It was greeted by a bit of gunfire from a villa on a promontory, a sort of advance post shrouded in vines. Fire was returned sporadically; they aimed for the windows, they hit the grapes. A corporal turned poet scribbled an ode to the landing in his notebook. They covered each other as they gradually made their way past the stronghold.

Simón advanced from rock to dune. He watched the villa, spotted the movement of Peruvian gunmen going window to window, spotted the lack of movement from the rattan chairs on the terrace. He dashed toward an overturned fishing boat that offered some cover, then a pile of seaweed, then crab traps.

Callao drew nearer; Simón would soon be able to blend in with its crowds, or its rubble, and make his way to the Ortuño residence. He studied the city once more, the black islands (oh, the windows) between the green rivers (oh, the vines); the changing positions of the Peruvians and the indifference of the parasols. He ran toward the city. He was taken for a target. A bullet rendered the dinghy unseaworthy, another dispatched a seashell … a third the corporal (oh, the humanity).

Simón reached the cover of the streets, wiped his brow with the back of his hand, and was surprised by how rough his sweat was. His palms didn't recognize the sandy skin: temples like sea urchins, rocky lips, pebbly beard leading to tragic questions, worry, anxiety – whose eyebrows of glistening ash are these? He took off his uniform, crept to the fountain near city hall and washed himself off. He looked twenty years younger. Still, in the water's reflection, he thought he looked old. So this is how it is, he thought. Love makes the heart young but the body old. And my mind is bouncing between sudden confidence and complete exhaustion. I have the fear, no the desire, wait, no, the fear of dying typical of adolescents and the elderly. It's what having too much time to think, or not enough time to think, can do to you.

❧

Wounded a fifth time, Admiral Núñez gave the signal to continue firing. Carry on, that's it, or we'll never be done. He had to suffer through the surgeon's exam once more: arm up, arm down, lie down, *bicycle* – what on earth? Come on, the doctor continued: legs up, move them in circles, thank you.

What made him endure the humiliation of the exam and, it

occurred to him, of his own ignorance, was the Plaza de Cibeles statue, which every bit of suffering brought him closer to.

He got up, leaning his weight on a barrel, just in time to witness, to the south, the *Villa de Madrid* being taken out of battle by a Blakely cannon. The shell made the boilers cough, releasing two or three black puffs, a sort of distress signal. Men came up on deck and spit blood before collapsing. Don't go down there. There was the explosion, and then the rain of crushed coal that sullied the dead, stung the living, attacking sailors like a cloud of bizarrely petrified insects.

There were rumours: thirty-five victims, the ship immobilized, the captain of the *Villa de Madrid* losing an arm trying to save the leg of a seaman caught under a girder. Núñez feared that the competition could rob him of his statue.

※

City hall was engulfed in flames. A human chain was passing buckets filled at the fountain. The lobby of the gutted building was wide open to view, along with the rhododendrons shrivelled from the heat, the mayor's office and the round portrait the smoke was already eating away at.

Simón was able to wind his way through the volunteer firefighters. He offered to go inside and see whether anyone was unconscious, didn't bother, and instead, quickly crossing the entire burnt-out ruins, slipped out a window at the back of the building. That way he avoided several checkpoints, barricades and a long detour. But not the mayor.

He grabbed Simón by the ankle, begging for help. What are you doing on your knees in your office? The smoke? No. The pain?

My good man, please.

He wasn't injured.

It was too heavy for one man alone, you see.

He wanted to save the portrait.

❧

As Núñez ordered the immobilized *Villa de Madrid* to be towed, a stray bullet wounded him for the sixth time. After the bicycle, he should have stayed lying on the deck. He was starting to worry his statue would be of the recumbent variety. He tried to get up using a barrel as support, tried again, fumed, in vain. Maybe this was how one earned immortality: looking up at the sky. He consoled himself. There must have been Roman emperors who had to think like him, lying prone and contemplative, no doubt less from the pain than from the laziness of the times.

His first mate described what Núñez couldn't see: two Spanish vessels retreating, at long last the dispatch of the Peruvian fleet that had started shelling. He made sure his commentary took the sting out of what he saw, to spare the wounded man. It was all without repercussions, inconsequential or purely routine. And Núñez watched the clouds, which looked like his silhouette, with his mount and his sword plain to see. The layer of clouds behind that depicted Madrid, or Rome.

❧

For fear of being recognized, Simón had ignored the mayor's pleas. His remorse at not having helped an art lover in distress was assuaged by his aesthetic sense. The portrait would be better off out of this world, preserved solely in memories that would embellish and descriptions that would lend it a bit of mystery. Who could say whether the painting, once it was gone and left to the devices of memory, would not become a work of art?

Simón came to the street he was looking for. The afternoon was fading, the battle along with it. Only sporadic gunfire and cries were exchanged. The sun was setting on the hills; the ruins of strongholds made strange geometric figures against their gentle slopes. A few flames punctuated the dusk, creating enough light to be able to make out a slight limp on a wounded shadow, the shadow of a rescuer, more shadows coming back down to the city to rest. Simón would have to be quick. The chaos of combat and therefore his camouflage were slowly but surely disappearing. Calm would be restored, with all of its danger.

Montse's house was the only one in the area destroyed. It offered passersby an almost perfect cross-section view. The front door was gone, as was the living room, for all intents and purposes. The sofa sat boldly enthroned on a pile of boards. The hallway with its shadows that used to cloak Montse's pallor had been transformed into a stage open onto the street, with no curtain. No actors either. The staircase was still holding, like a snake charmed by the emptiness, rising up to meet the remains of the second floor — beams, a room suspended in the air.

Simón thought again of the heaviest rocks on the most fragile body parts, felt a jolt in his heart, then it waned, then he was angry, and finally sick. He ran toward the house to avoid throwing up. He started searching through the debris, tore his clothes, tried to find a body he could cry over in the dust and the rubble.

He felt a hand on his shoulder. Smooth with delicate joints, lily white, manicured nails – he felt a spark of hope.

Slowly, he turned his head.

The hair was in a chignon, the chin was double.

It was the Ortuños' maid.

Eyes glazed with sorrow stared at Simón, white like two hosts. Blink, would you? Her round face was covered in soot. She blinked:

only her eyelids were clean. Can you hear me? She had the disquieting look of a great grey owl, with the colours reversed, its plumage mixed up, moon eyes and night face. Everything in this country is backward.

Mademoiselle had already left with her brother for the hacienda when the shelling began.

There's no point in digging, the maid murmured. Well, maybe for the cutlery or the oak sideboard that are down there, if you really want them.

And her bedroom?

That's what's still holding on the second floor; that's what's suspended, her bedroom.

Simón moved toward the staircase – careful, it's not safe – and then went up – the stairs are collapsing, you see. He listened to the maid's cries and the wood cracking. Come back, Sir, come back, there's no point in going up there. Simón studied each of the stairs, stepped across those that wouldn't hold his foot while clinging to great, hanging swaths of wallpaper to steady himself.

Finally he entered the bedroom, which was unstable. It was like being in a tree, in a treehouse, the curious feeling of childlike seclusion that was rather pleasing. The loss of several joists gave the floor more spring. The weight of the bed made it sag dangerously and turned one corner of the bedroom into a sort of giant hammock. Burns dotted her sheets, as if embers had slept on them, or someone had smoked copiously and negligently.

The small table was still in front of the window, the frame of which was shaky but hanging on in a half-collapsed wall. Simón went to it to look out over the bay.

The sea was filled with Spanish ships, some of them in flames, others with broken masts that looked like arms punished for having wanted to touch, let's say, the sky. No, that's not it. How about punished for having wanted to avoid getting wet, having gotten wet. It was foolish to hope to stay dry, yes, that's it. Hope, foolishness, life.

Simón realized that the Spanish fleet was packing up its cannonballs. The ships were slowly shrinking in the distance. Soon they would be too far to reach. Good, he said to himself, we're leaving. Love ends as war ends.

He looked down at the table. A psychology book was open on it. *The human mind contains all worlds, except the one we live in.*

Simón closed his eyes, concentrated, concentrated some more, looked through the window again. Nothing had changed. Except the ships, which were becoming indistinct shapes. He picked up the book and left in its place the most beautiful letter ever written. He hoped that the bedroom would survive, that it would hold, suspended like this, until Montse's return, so that she would know that he had been there, see that her book had disappeared, notice the . . .

No. The letter was too much: pompous, fleeting, the words, the seal, to say nothing of the salt and the blood. He took it back – it was madness. The book's absence would be enough.

He turned on his heel, clung to the wallpaper and, at the bottom of the stairs, thanked the maid. She seemed sorry. She had seen Montse's face as she left for Lambayeque. You have the same look on your face, she said, the same! Where are your eyes?

He said his goodbyes and walked slowly down the middle of the street. His shadow followed him.

The maid knelt in the rubble. She watched him go and, telling herself that someone should, she cried. Poor children who do not know how to suffer, who do not know how to change the course of destiny. Poor children swept along by the century. You sleep. You sleep and you die.

Her tears washed her face. They turned black, soaking up the soot, and left white rivers in their path.

The sun, which was setting, still stained the horizon blue; the main part of the battle was over. Simón, accompanied by a few saboteurs who had survived the operation, rowed in the direction of the Spanish ships that were clustered on the horizon.

They were tallying losses, examining the hulls, counting the wounds Admiral Núñez had sustained. One, two, three … a bit of quiet please, one, two, three … hurrah! The sailors' joy kept interrupting the doctor's attempts to count. Spain has conquered, dear doctor; come on, a bit of enthusiasm, Admiral, no? Tousled, dishevelled heads leaned over the wounded man. Núñez was patient.

The other side were congratulating themselves as well, for having staved off the invasion, for having died for the cause, for having saved the mayor's portrait at the eleventh hour.

Calls of *Viva Peru* rose from the far side of the bay, came down from the hilltops, reached the retreating ships. It was a bombardment of voices that perpetuated the hostilities. Núñez, whose pain made him intransigent, believed this enthusiasm to be unwarranted.

After all, it was Spain that had regained her standing, was it not? There was smoke rising from the coast, and buildings were collapsing in the city. And we never even wanted to invade the place. It was to punish South America and impress Europe.

Americans were contemplating the scene on sea and on land: a painter, a businessman and a commodore. They commented on the course of events. Over so quickly and the damage to the city was minimal. Quite right, Mr. Rodgers, I would even venture that the Peruvian batteries contained Núñez so effectively that he wasn't able to shell its infrastructures. Nicely done.

Yes.

Yes.

Basically, they were joining the citizens of Callao in their calls of *Viva* and in cursing imperialism.

It's untrue, patently untrue, Núñez would defend himself months later in Madrid. The city was hit hard, Callao was ravaged. I am told that the city hall went up in flames. And that at least one house was destroyed.

He scratched his sideburns. He had been wounded nine times. Well done, Mr. Núñez.

But there was no mention of a statue.

※

For the time being, Núñez ordered his men to set a course for San Lorenzo Island. It was Peru's largest island, opposite Callao; its highest point – at 396 metres above sea level – gave them a view of enemy movements and other minute geographical details, and they could repair their ships there.

Hoisted aboard the *Villa de Madrid*, Simón paced the decks. He wrote while walking, crossed out while standing, continued writing the report of his expedition, omitting a good number of details – the mayor's whimpering, the maid's whimpering, his own whimpering, which he replaced with cool and calm. But his report could wait. The captain, now a one-armed man, was fighting for his life; the ship, which was hit in the bilge, was fighting to stay afloat. So much fighting, and yet the crew was basking in the sun. Having sealed the hull, bailing the hold every half-hour, they let themselves be gently towed. We'll play cards, bet with matches, watch Callao disappear in the distance. And hey, we should ask Simón about his mission.

So, Lieutenant?

Nothing.

Rape?

Not by me.

And the lady?, those who were in on it asked. The gentlewoman? Did you see her?

Simón explained that he had found her dead under a pile of debris and that now, if you please, he would pace the deck at night like a ghost and shut himself away in his cabin during the day like a madman. Never again would he look for love. He had lost the heart. His heart was buried next to the woman, where it was budding to make her a tree, a tomb, some shade. So leave me alone now, it's over.

But Lieutenant, was she still beautiful in death?

Was she wearing a nightie?

Was she naked?

17

In San Lorenzo, they were able to repair the ships well enough and enjoy the beach a little. Then the island became more dangerous, and the war more difficult:

1. The allied fleet was gathering.
2. Spanish morale was flagging.
3. The beach was no Costa Brava.
4. They had no source of supplies.

All the South American ports were now closed to them. The chart at the back of the cabin was scarred with red Xs: where they had been turned away, hostile territory and a treasure that the natives had spoken of, or at least one native. Núñez smoked, and then smoked some more, but he could still see the crimson marks through the haze, showing past operations and pointing to future obstacles. The conflict cannot be redone, Núñez thought. To persist would require scribbling too many borders, oceans, cities. Out-and-out war, a semi-world war. It was unthinkable.

And anyway, they had already restored some of their honour, almost enough.

He scratched his sideburns, left his cabin and went to address his men on deck. His forehead and his eyes were haloed by a cloud of grey smoke; only his mouth could be seen clearly. It twitched, whispered, couldn't form the words and then could: he ordered the return to Spain. We'll pick everyone up at the Chincha Islands, maybe a mollusc specimen or two for the Academy of Science, and then we'll be back in Madrid.

Núñez went back to his tobacco, was sad, was nervous, sat down, stood up and dreamed. He ripped the chart from the wall. He fed his pipe little pieces of South America until late in the night. Nine wounds. Who could deny him a statue?

So they went back to the Chincha Islands. The few garrisons that had been left there were glad to be back on board. Their uniforms were covered with what looked like a layer of cracking grey stucco. Yet they had taken care of them, they swore, as well as they could. But even the water was dubiously clean, always greasy, always black and impenetrable, as if drawn from the bottom of a well.

Although the locals drank it – but then look at their fish eyes, pupils clouded, never clear, as murky as the bottom of a well – in fact, so dark they scare you, Captain, Admiral, Lieutenant, endlessly damning you; it's as if they're looking past you, as if you are a mere spectre, a mere vibration, and they're looking right through you.

Anything else?

The eyes of a bat, there.

They were stuck on the islands for a few days with nothing to do. They disembarked from the ships to stretch their legs and throw rocks at the terns. They awaited their departure, thinking of Madrid. They watched the people who, left with few masters, were doing nothing as well. They hid away in the houses, shutters closed, they went out to draw water from the fountain, disappeared into the countryside, alone, and came back in pairs or not at all.

As for Núñez, he hesitated, scratched and smoked. He asked that they get fresh supplies from what they could find; very well, they said, plants along the roadside, lichen, igneous rocks, a bit of greasy water?

There were rumblings that it would be impossible to go back without stopping, the lack of provisions, the closing of South American ports. Núñez would find a way, so have patience, everyone. As long as he smoked: patience.

As the fantasy of a woman to sequester and undress started to fade, Simón no longer appreciated the islands as much. He observed the ashy walls, the ashy skin; the sky seemed to be stained with ash, pale grey or grey-green, sometimes dark grey. He paced the village, noting a few morose, strange details in his notebook. A new grey here, a three-armed child there. Everyone was watching him. Dilated pupils shifted back and forth between the shutters; discussions were interrupted in the square, and resumed in whispers. He liked to go to the fountain, sit down and write, all day long, about the disquieting shifts in the silence.

Sometimes a local came to draw some greasy water and greeted him as if alerting him to danger. He would leave, looking back over his shoulder.

An entire secret society was percolating beneath the surface of this weariness, Simón scribbled, a sort of shameful cadaver was decomposing, fermenting, in the quiet, tomb-like houses. A village tragedy, the curse of ancestors, seemed to hover over the place, which, truth be told, took him a long way from the rationality of the war, and entertained him.

And then, one day, something bad indeed happened. A corpse was found lying at the foot of the fountain. Someone had taken the trouble to excise the eyelids so the eyes would find no rest. Black blood oozed from below the eyebrows. It pooled on the cheeks before trickling down to the rock, mixing with the shit to form a brownish paste. The eyes lost in death, Simón observed, went straight through him – dear spectre, mere vibration – continuing their dark contemplation through his body, as if he didn't exist. It was the three-armed child.

Now no one wanted to leave the ship, and it was becoming urgent that Núñez make a decision. Simón had noted everything about his misadventure; it could come in handy, a gothic South American story, a bestseller in Madrid, the climax of a travelogue. He may even have written the first line of a novel.

Then Montse returned, settled in, haunted him in any fanciful form: lunar, aviary, capillary and finally philosophical. It was the secret book lying on the work table: he had wanted to work, and he had seen it. He had read the first sentence, the next one, read up to the sentence that she liked so much, to understand its significance.

And he read, with the most beautiful letter ever written serving as a bookmark. He imagined himself reaching her thoughts and her words a little. He wondered whether she was slowly forgetting him, if their memories were tugging on each other and bringing each other back to life in a sort of invisible to and fro, or at some point made contact to form just one; or if instead they wandered through two lands that Simón and Montse visited all on their own.

He was interrupted by a seaman.

Lieutenant, he explained, Núñez has spoken. There was divinatory smoke and a solemn mouth. The return journey? Not Cape Horn, a wild idea, a radical solution. What, then? Green beaches, brown nipples. Don't be coarse, Simón interrupted. Blue hair, floral necklaces, honey-coloured hair, grass skirts, raven hair, silk dragons, chocolate-brown hair, flasks of spices, who knows, love in one of these hues. The Port of Hong Kong, it seems. Get a hold of yourself, Simón said firmly. Foreign lands, strange countries, the Port of Chittagong. Please, Simón finally took offence. End, full stop.

Then, all the same, out of curiosity:

Hair the colour of dead leaves?

And since he had been told that the return journey would take the Spanish fleet around the world, the sailor added, my lieutenant, imagine whatever you like.

Louis Carmain is from Québec City. *Guano* is his first novel, and it received the prestigious Prix des Collégiens. *Bunyip*, his second novel, was published in 2014.

Rhonda Mullins is a writer and translator living in Montréal. *And the Birds Rained Down*, her translation of Jocelyne Saucier's *Il pleuvait des oiseaux*, was a CBC Canada Reads Selection. It was also shortlisted for the Governor General's Literary Award, as were her translations of Élise Turcotte's *Guyana* and Hervé Fischer's *The Decline of the Hollywood Empire*.

Typeset in Albertan

Albertan was designed by the late Jim Rimmer of New Westminster, B.C., in 1982. He drew and cut the type in metal at the 16pt size in roman only; it was intended for use only at his Pie Tree Press. He drew the italic in 1985, designing it with a narrow fit and a very slight incline, and created a digital version. The family was completed in 2005, when Rimmer redrew the bold weight and called it Albertan Black. The letterforms of this type family have an old-style character, with Rimmer's own calligraphic hand in evidence, especially in the italic.

Printed at the old Coach House on bpNichol Lane in Toronto, Ontario, on Rolland Natural paper, which was manufactured, acid-free, in Saint-Jérôme, Quebec, from second-growth forests. This book was printed with vegetable-based ink on a 1965 Heidelberg KORD offset litho press. Its pages were folded on a Baumfolder, gathered by hand, bound on a Sulby Auto-Minabinda and trimmed on a Polar single-knife cutter.

Edited and designed by Alana Wilcox
Cover by Ingrid Paulson

Coach House Books
80 bpNichol Lane
Toronto ON M5S 3J4
Canada

416 979 2217
800 367 6360

mail@chbooks.com
www.chbooks.com